Luscious
Love

Luscious Love

KATERINA BAKOLIAS

JAMES LORIMER & COMPANY LTD., PUBLISHERS
TORONTO

James Lorimer & Company Ltd., Publishers acknowledges funding support from the Ontario Arts Council (OAC), an agency of the Government of Ontario. We acknowledge the support of the Canada Council for the Arts. This project has been made possible in part by the Government of Canada and with the support of Ontario Creates.

Cover design: Tyler Cleroux
Cover image: iStock, Shutterstock

Library and Archives Canada Cataloguing in Publication

Title: Luscious love / Katerina Bakolias.
Names: Bakolias, Katerina, author.
Series: RealLove.
Description: Series statement: Real love
Identifiers: Canadiana (print) 2023053547X | Canadiana (ebook) 20230535488 | ISBN 9781459418066 (hardcover) | ISBN 9781459418059 (softcover) | ISBN 9781459418073 (EPUB)
Subjects: LCGFT: Romance fiction. | LCGFT: Novels.
Classification: LCC PS8603.A462 L87 2024 | DDC jC813/.6—dc23

Published by:
James Lorimer &
Company Ltd., Publishers
117 Peter Street, Suite 304
Toronto, ON, Canada
M5V 0M3
www.lorimer.ca

Distributed in Canada by:
Formac Lorimer Books
5502 Atlantic Street
Halifax, NS, Canada
B3H 1G4
www.formaclorimerbooks.ca

Distributed in the US by:
Lerner Publisher Services
241 1st Ave. N.
Minneapolis, MN, USA
55401
www.lernerbooks.com

Printed and bound in Canada

For Rosalia — may you always know you're worthy of love.

01 First Day on the Job

CLOTHES WERE SCATTERED all over Mina's bedroom floor, some flung across her bed, and what remained in the closet was half-hanging. How could she have so much clothing and not a single thing to wear on her first day? Mina stood in front of the mirror on the back of her bedroom door, a place she normally hated to be, but today was different. Today was her first day as a sales associate at Luscious Lingerie, and she wanted to pick out the perfect outfit. The dress code was all black, Mina's favourite colour. She'd settled on a pair of black leggings, a black cami, and a cropped black knit cardigan. She turned to the side and inspected her outfit, adding a simple pair of gold earrings and pulling her curly black hair back into a ponytail. *Comfy, practical, and cute,* she thought with a smile. She wasn't usually the type to focus so much on her appearance, but she wanted to look the part.

Mina hurried downstairs. Her older brother and sister, Dimitri and Alexandra, were already sitting at the kitchen table eating breakfast. Her mother, Voula, stood at the counter preparing some phyllo pastry. Although she'd been up for hours, she hurried around the kitchen with an energy that made it impossible to know if she was having fun or running around in complete and utter panic. Voula was the type of woman who had an opinion about everything and a solution for every problem.

"I've been calling you for an hour," her mother said, looking up from the counter. "Is that what you're wearing?"

"Ma!" Mina rolled her eyes and inspected her outfit again.

"What?" Voula sighed as she threw her hands in the air. "I can't ask a question?"

"You look fine," Alexandra called from the table, annoyed at the early-morning commotion.

Mina poured herself a cup of coffee and sat down. "I'd like to look more than *fine* for my first day," she muttered under her breath.

"And you do," Alexandra assured her. "Right, Ma?"

"Yes, yes, now eat. Eat," Voula said as she placed a plate of fresh bread on the table.

"Oh, is it your first day at a new internship for the National Bank? Did you beat out fifty other applicants to earn your spot?" Dimitri chirped. "No, wait, that's me." He puffed up his chest and grinned while shoving a whole hard-boiled egg into his mouth. Mina rolled her eyes, and Alexandra ignored him.

"So many firsts today." Their father Yiannis beamed as he waltzed into the room with his backpack flung over his shoulder. "I'm very proud." He kissed each of his children on the tops of their heads before kissing Voula on the lips and pouring himself a cup of coffee.

Mina's father never wore a sweater with fewer than five pockets, he never spent money on extra things (his wallet was just an elastic band wrapped around his bank cards), and he always told his family that he was proud of them. Yiannis pulled out his phone, opened the camera app, and held it up over his head. "Let's get a family selfie." Everyone groaned but leaned in for the photo. He had a whole album on his phone dedicated to family selfies that featured his forehead in the front with the rest of the family scattered in the background.

At last, the whole family sat down to eat. Mina looked at the delicious spread on the table: sliced fruit, toast, a bowl of hard-boiled eggs, and feta cheese. She filled her plate and began eating. Her mother sat down beside her and swiped a piece of bread off Mina's plate. Before Mina could protest, her mother's phone rang.

It was louder than an ambulance driving through the middle of their living room.

Voula answered the phone and launched into a conversation in Greek. Mina continued to eat, defiantly taking another piece of bread and slathering it with jam. She could tell that her aunt, Thea Georgia, was on the other end of the call. She heard her sister's name and assumed they were talking about her recent acceptance into medical school.

But who knows? It's all Greek to me, Mina thought, *literally.*

She understood some of what her parents said. They had been committed to teaching their kids Greek, that is until the Greek Church changed their lessons from Wednesday nights to Friday nights, which conflicted with Alexandra's soccer practices. And once Dimitri came along they had to drive in two nights a week for level 1 and level 2 Greek courses. So by the time Mina entered the family picture, things were too hectic and they'd given up. One day she would learn, especially since she planned to travel to Greece, and knowing the language would make it much easier to get around.

Thea Georgia and her mother were always fussing over whose kids were doing what, who was getting this award, who was accepted onto what sports team, who was going to be the first one in the family to get married, and on and on. Mina tried not to worry about it. She wasn't smart and popular like her sister or athletic and charismatic like her brother, so her name didn't come up much in those conversations.

"Your Thea wishes you good luck," her mother said when she finally hung up.

"Thanks," Mina and Dimitri said at the same time, glaring at one another.

Once breakfast was done, Mina ran upstairs to grab her purse and pick out a nice pair of black shoes to match her outfit. She looked at herself one more time in the mirror, not sure if she now hated the outfit she'd chosen earlier. She placed her hand on her stomach and squeezed. She knew she had a belly; she wasn't blind, but she didn't know why having one had to consume so much of her thoughts. In a weird way it seemed like other people were constantly reminding her to focus on it.

Or is it just me? She turned to face the mirror again and tugged at the cropped cardigan. *Maybe I should change into a sweater that covers my stomach . . .*

"Mina, let's go!" Dimitri called from downstairs.

Too late, she thought. Dimitri agreed to drive her to work on his way to the bank. She hated driving in his dingy little Honda Civic with the embarrassing black spoiler on the back, but it was better than taking the bus. She took one last look at her room and sighed, knowing she had a huge mess to clean up later. Then she hurried down the stairs and out the front door, where her brother was waiting for her.

On the drive over, Mina scrolled through the @LusciousLingerie Instagram account. They had over two million followers, both fashion icons and regular women. While they posted pictures and videos of the Lush Models, as they called them, and their products, they also posted photos of their employees from all around the world. *Lushes* was the unofficial title the employees gave themselves.

"Ugh, don't tell me you're trying to be a TikTok star," Dimitri spat after quickly glancing at Mina's phone.

"No. What do you care anyway?" Mina retorted.

"I don't, but Mom and Dad would freak." He chuckled.

"Whatever," Mina scoffed, "keep your eyes on the road."

"I'm just saying, Mom and Dad expect more from you." He shrugged and leaned back in the driver's seat. Mina rolled her eyes. She loved her brother, but sometimes he was such an ass.

02

Here, There, and Underwear

THE MALL PARKING LOT was packed. It was the first day of summer break, and everyone was at the waterfront, the beach, or the mall. Dimitri dropped Mina off at the main doors, so she had to walk through the mall to get to Luscious Lingerie. She kept her head down to avoid any awkward run-ins with the kids she went to school with.

Mina kept to herself most of the time. She had a couple of good friends that she'd known since elementary school, but that was it. She wasn't popular.

Not like her sister, who never seemed uncomfortable in social situations. Or her brother, who could make new friends anywhere. It was so embarrassing to start high school and have everyone refer to her as Alexandra's little sister. After that, Mina knew that no matter what she did in class, it wouldn't be good enough. Expectations were high — too high. She felt like people assumed she would do exactly what Alexandra did: step one, become a star soccer player on the school's varsity team. Step two, get top marks. Step three, finish it all off by being crowned prom queen.

Well, that wasn't Mina. She was shy and quiet, she didn't take to sports like her siblings did, and she didn't really like school. She'd rather spend her time listening to true crime podcasts, reading travel blogs, or exploring new hiking trails. She wanted to make her own way, and getting a part-time job at Luscious Lingerie was the first step. She just had to save enough money for her first year of college. Then she'd start putting money away to travel, something no one in her family seemed interested in doing.

Mina stood outside of Luscious Lingerie, admiring the large displays of beautiful women posed in lace panties and frilly bras. She made her way through the store, past the towering panty displays and the drawers filled with bras for every occasion, and approached the counter. The glittery floor tiles sparkled under the elegant ceiling lights. Each section of the store was like entering a new world. There was a sports section with an industrial feel, a swimwear section that looked like a hotel lobby in Cancun, and three other sections devoted to the different types of bras that they sold.

"Hi, I'm Mina. I'm new." Mina held out her hand to the girl working at the cash. The girl looked Mina up and down and pointed to the door behind the counter.

"Training's happening in the back," the cranky cashier replied.

Mina took her hand back and carefully stepped behind the counter. She opened the door to the backroom and slowly poked her head in. Monica, the woman who had interviewed and hired Mina, was chatting with an Asian girl about Mina's age.

"Mina! Come on in!" Monica welcomed her into the space. There was a real difference between the store and the backroom; none of the frills, beauty, and fashion had made its way into the back offices of Luscious Lingerie. It reminded Mina of her school's cafeteria. Fluorescent lighting, dirty tiled floors, a vending machine, and a few tables and chairs set up near a microwave and coffee machine.

"Thanks," Mina said as she sat down next to the other girl.

"I'm Serena." The girl leaned over and shook Mina's hand with a smile. *Thank goodness.* Mina relaxed a little and smiled back. Serena looked like a model herself. She was tall, lean, and had the shiniest hair Mina had ever seen.

"I am so excited to start your onboarding!" Monica was practically bouncing off the walls. "You two beat out so many other applicants. I mean, I don't have to tell you how coveted our positions are." She laughed. The door to the break room swung open, and the cranky cashier stomped inside.

"Monica, I'm clocking out," she groaned as she grabbed her things.

"No problem, sweetie. I'll come check you out." Monica left with the cashier, then returned a moment later. "Sorry about that. We have to do checkouts at the end of everyone's shift. I'll explain it all later. It's her last day." Monica sighed. "She started off really great, but I don't know what happened . . . Anyway, let's review your onboarding package!"

Monica explained the company's history, its humble beginnings to its billion-dollar empire, and most importantly, she stressed the company's slogan, "striving for excellence." They watched training videos, did short quizzes, and read the employee handbook. Next was a tour of the store and product testing. Monica took them through the store and "introduced" them to their three best-selling bras as if they were actual people. Each bra had its own special section of the store with its own merchandise, matching panties, sleep sets, perfume, lotion, and more.

"Meet the Everyday Bra." Monica led them into a section of the store that was set up to look like the closet of a modern woman on the go. It had fake windows that looked out onto a cityscape, and photos of models wearing matching pyjamas and getting ready to take on the day. It was almost inspiring. "Each bra has its own matching panty because we want to offer our customers the complete comfort set. You might not have your life together, but matching your underwear to your bra will always make you feel better." Monica placed her hand on her heart as if she'd passed on a piece of very wise advice.

Next, the Push-Up Bra had its own section near the back of the store. The walls were a dark purple and the images of the models were much sexier and more serious than the other sections. Lastly, the Fantasy Bra had a special place near the front of the store. It had the most delicate designs as seen in Luscious Lingerie's fashion shows, Instagram, and basically any tall, thin female celebrity's social media pages.

"We have so much to offer our customer base.

With such a diverse palate, we're able to give women what they really want: confidence. That's what we do here, we make women feel good about themselves."

Mina couldn't help but smile as they made their way back to the staff room. This was exactly what she was hoping for: to make women feel good in their bodies. An opportunity to feel good in her own body. *I mean, they wouldn't have hired me if they didn't think I was Luscious material, right?*

Mina scooted behind the counter and caught the eye of the new cashier starting her shift, Lexie. Mina recognized her from school. Her breath caught in her throat, and a sudden rush of anxiety swept over her. *Lexie works here.*

Lexie Hayes was the lead in their high school musical. She won an award for her marks in AP Computer Science, and she was always invited out to parties with the popular kids — not that Mina would know if she actually went to the parties, never having been invited herself. But still! Lexie was so confident and beautiful.

Oh no, and I'm an impostor, Mina thought in a panic. *She's going to know I don't belong here.* She held her breath and hoped that Lexie wouldn't notice her.

"Lexie, sweetie," Monica called in her sing-song voice, "thank you so much for jumping on cash today! We owe you one."

"You owe me like twenty!" Lexie laughed, making Monica laugh as she went into the break room.

"Hey, Mina, right?" Lexie said, stopping Mina in her tracks.

"Yeah, that's right," Mina choked.

"Lexie. We went to school together." Lexie smiled, trying to jog Mina's memory.

"Yeah, of course," Mina blurted out. "I know. I mean, hi. It's great to see you."

Lexie smiled at Mina's babbling and tucked her hair behind her ears. "You too," she chimed and returned to work.

Mina followed Monica and Serena back into the staff room and sat down. Her face was flushed, and she felt sweaty.

"Okay, the last thing we have to cover for today is the different positions available." Monica flipped through her papers. Serena gently raised her hand and waited to be called on.

Monica gave her a nod, and she proceeded with her question. "I thought we were hired as sales associates?"

"Well, there are a couple positions available. Sales associate is one of them, but we'll have to see if you're the right fit. There's also merchandising, cash, and fitting rooms. Oh! And we have to talk about dress code." Monica gave a little finger-wag to Mina as she eyed her leggings. "Striving for excellence, remember? Sales associates are expected to wear dress pants. No jeans and no leggings. No low-cut tops. Think business professional. So no colourful hair dye, no facial jewelry like nose rings, no visible tattoos. We want our employees to have a clean, chic look. And it's mandatory to wear underwear — preferably Luscious brand."

"How would you even enforce that?" Mina wondered out loud. Monica puckered her lips, as though she had sucked on a lemon. "Sorry," Mina mumbled.

Then Monica laughed and continued. "The better you know the product, the better you'll be able to help our customers find exactly what they need," Monica said. "And don't worry, you'll get a thirty percent discount on everything."

At the end of the day, Monica hugged them both and welcomed them to the Luscious Lingerie family. She gave them each a voucher for a free bra and panty. Mina was so excited and decided to hang around and shop after her shift. Monica helped her clock out, which meant logging out on the store computer then having a bag check — where Monica looked through Mina's purse to make sure she didn't steal anything. That felt weird to Mina, but Monica assured her it was a standard practice.

Mina browsed the shelves and stopped when she came upon the "Panty Drawer," as Monica had called it. It was a huge display table with thirty different kinds of underwear in every colour and pattern you could imagine in the drawers underneath.

"It takes a while, but eventually you'll get used to saying it." Lexie appeared with an armful of bras.

"What?" Mina asked, surprised to see Lexie again.

"*Panty*," Lexie explained with a laugh. "It's such an uncomfortable word to say, but you'll get used to it."

"Oh! Yeah, kind of like *moist*." Mina chuckled.

"That one doesn't bother me as much." Lexie shrugged.

"Really? I hate it. More than the word *panty* . . . Ugh, now that I've said it out loud though . . ."

"How was your first day?" Lexie moved around Mina, putting bras away in their proper drawers divided by size and style.

"It was . . . good," Mina decided.

"It's a lot of material to cover, but don't overthink it," Lexie reassured her. "You'll be great. Any idea which department they're going to stick you in?"

"Not sure yet. Sales, or maybe cash," Mina added hopefully.

"Nah, you want to do merchandising and stock, trust me." Lexie leaned against the panty drawers and eyed the pieces that Mina had picked out.

"Aren't you a cashier?"

"Me? No. I was just filling in for Andrea. It was her last day today, and she could only work half her shift, so I covered the second half."

"Oh." Mina assumed she was referring to the rude cashier from earlier.

"I'm on the stock team. I do some merchandising too," Lexie said as she started folding panties piled up on the table in front of them.

"Well, maybe I'll check that out then." Mina could feel her cheeks burning.

"You should." Lexie smiled.

She has an amazing smile, Mina thought. *She's so beautiful. Uh-oh.* She could feel her heart pounding a little harder. *Na-uh, we're not going to go about catching feelings for the beautiful, cool girl you work with. Calm down!*

Her reverse pep talk didn't work. Lexie gave her a confused look, and Mina realized that she hadn't said anything in the last few seconds. She stood there awkwardly, trying to think of something to say. Instead, she held up her arm full of bras and waved them around as if she was giving Lexie an explanation of why she couldn't speak.

"You wanna try those on?" Lexie asked, one eyebrow raised and a slight smile tugging at her mouth.

"Umm, ahh, yes, please . . . " she floundered.

"Sure, I'll open a fitting room for you." Lexie led her back into the fitting rooms, which looked like the inside of Barbie's dream house: pink walls, chandeliers, cushions, and elegant doors.

"So, you work the fitting rooms too, huh?" Mina tried to make a joke.

"Nah, but I know where they keep the keys." Lexie winked as she opened a dressing room for Mina. "Holler if you need anything!"

How about a new personality? Mina thought as she closed the dressing room door and slumped against the wall. *I could use a new one. . . .*

03 The Perfect Fit

WHEN MINA GOT HOME, after a twenty-minute bus ride, her mother was rushing around the kitchen getting dinner ready. Voula threw a dishcloth over her shoulder and hugged Mina.

"Tell me about your first day," she demanded.

"It was good." Mina nodded.

"Good? Just good? The job you've been talking about nonstop for weeks was just *good*? What did they do to you? Huh?" Her mother rambled, getting more and more excited with each question. "I hope you're not spending your whole paycheque on your first day." She pointed to the shopping bag in Mina's hand.

"Huh? Oh, no, they gave me a free bra and some . . . underwear," Mina explained, avoiding the word *panty.* She showed her mother her new bra, a very practical choice that Voula approved of, and told her all about the training. Her mother asked her questions and even seemed interested in getting some new undergarments now that Mina had a discount.

"We could go shopping together. And once I've learned how to do a fitting I could help find you something," Mina gushed.

"Perfect." Voula kissed Mina on the cheek and went back to peeling potatoes. Mina never got to spend any time alone with her mother. There was always someone else demanding attention. "Then we pick you a bra that gets you a boyfriend," her mother added.

And then Mina remembered why she didn't spend much time with her mother. Were all mothers so focused on marrying off their daughters? Or was it just Greek mothers?

Just then, Dimitri walked in the door and began to tell their mom all about his first day at the bank. Apparently he'd been shadowing the manager instead of one of the clerks, like he thought, and this made him feel all the more self-important. Mina had no trouble slipping away to her room.

Shit, she thought as she turned on her bedroom light, *what a mess*. She'd forgotten the state she left her room in this morning. She threw her phone and purse onto her bed and started picking up her clothes. She didn't know if what Monica said was true, that wearing matching underwear would always make you feel better. But she knew that having a clean space always made her feel like she had her life together. Haven't studied for your exam yet? Better clean your room first, that'll make you study better. No prom date? No problem. Clean your room. Stressed about a family get together? Clean your room so you have a neat place to cry in when you get home. It didn't really make sense, but Mina didn't need to understand it to know that it worked. Although she did wonder if her parents had somehow brainwashed her.

Finally, once her room was tidy, she hopped onto her bed and unlocked her phone. A new notification flashed on her feed:

@LexieLikesTrouble has started following you on Instagram.

Mina sucked in her breath and immediately checked out the account. Yup, it was Lexie. She quickly followed her back and started scrolling through her photos. There were lots of selfies, some pictures of her at the beach in a bikini that Mina recognized from Luscious Lingerie, and a few artsy nature photos.

Lexie was beautiful. She had this attitude like she would tell you honestly what she thought of you, but wouldn't care what you think of her. Mina always admired her in school. She just seemed like the kind of person who did what she wanted, got along with everyone easily, and didn't realize how cool they actually were.

Mina bit her lip looking at a photo of Lexie from last summer. Her hair was long, and she was lifting it off her shoulders in this sort of half movement, like she was stepping toward the camera but looking away at the same time. It could have been a professional photo with Lexie posing so effortlessly. *Should I like it?*

Her thumb hovered over the button. It was a pretty classic move to go through someone's Instagram page and like an old photo to let them know you were checking them out. *Hm . . . no. YES. No! Yes.* Mina double-tapped the picture and practically threw her phone across the room. It landed with thud on her bedroom floor, and she scrambled to pick it up.

"What are you doing?" her mother yelled from downstairs.

"Nothing!" Mina yelled as she rolled off her bed and onto the floor. She grabbed her phone and inspected it. Thankfully, it wasn't broken.

"It doesn't sound like nothing," Voula retorted.

Ping! Mina's heart stopped. A new notification flashed across her screen. A message from @LexieLikesTrouble: *Hey, how's it going?*

Her next shift at Luscious Lingerie was only a few days later, but Mina could hardly wait to be back at work. She and Lexie had started texting nonstop. Mina was surprised to discover that Lexie was nice, and funny, and actually enjoyed lots of the same things Mina did. Going in for her second shift felt easier knowing there was a friend waiting for her.

Today, Monica was determined to find out which position suited Mina best and decided they would start with sales associate. She told Mina to go sell some bras and described her teaching method as "a trial by fire." The phrase made Mina's stomach sink. Monica insisted that because it was the most desired of all the Luscious Lingerie positions, she could only trust associates who had a natural talent for it.

So Mina did as she was told. She found it comforting to see Lexie putting new product out and running around to the different sections of the store. Mina was assigned to work in the Everyday

Bra section, where she wandered around the tables, tidying up, greeting customers, and offering to help them whenever they were nearby. It was weird; some people wanted to have Mina walk around with them the entire time they were shopping, and others just ignored her. One such customer stomped back over moments later to ask, in a very annoyed tone, where Mina was hiding the perfume. Mina showed her where it was with a smile, remembering her training — the customer is always right — even though the customer accused her of moving the perfume from where they usually kept it. Mina just nodded along. It was only her second day, so how was she supposed to know if they'd moved it two feet from where it was before? She tried to shrug it off and returned to her section.

Several times she noticed Monica out of the corner of her eye hiding behind a mannequin or ducking behind a nearby table. Mina wasn't entirely sure if she was trying to watch her work or if she was avoiding customers. Not long after the perfume incident, another sales associate who looked like she stepped right off a runway in Paris snapped at her for "poaching" one of her customers. Mina apologized and tried to explain that the customer had approached *her* with a question, but Monica stepped in before things got too heated.

"Sales associates are very serious about their customer relationships. Once you build a strong bond with someone, it's almost heartbreaking to see them shopping with someone else, you know." Another piece of advice from Monica.

"Right. Yeah." Mina nodded. "I guess the commission's worth fighting for."

"Oh, it's not about the money." Monica shook her head.

"So how am I doing?" Mina asked, feeling the need to change the subject.

"Mmmmmm," Monica hummed in a high-pitched voice as she pursed her lips.

04 *The Anxiety Snake*

MONICA GOT MINA SET UP ON CASH. She walked her through a transaction and then let her do a few practice ones on her own. It was pretty simple. Mina got a flashback to the plastic toy cash register her parents got her for Christmas when she was eight. Funny to think that they made toys like that. Once Mina got the hang of it, Monica left her to ring through customers on her own.

This might be the place for me, she thought. It was repetitive, there was no upselling or commission to fight over, and people were generally pleased with their purchases. Until a woman who looked like she had a permanent frown approached the counter.

"I'd like to return this," she said as she placed a bag with three pairs of underwear inside it on the counter.

"Sure, I just have to call my manager — "

"I didn't ask to speak to your manager. I asked you to return these panties," the woman snapped. Mina flinched at the word *panties.*

"Right, but —"

"But there's no receipt. Look, I don't need a receipt. I was here last week, I wore these once, and then they shrank in the wash. Is that the kind of product you people sell here? Huh? Garbage?" She slapped her hands down on the counter to emphasize her point.

Mina was silent for a moment, unsure how to react to this grown woman yelling at her about underwear. She could feel the anxiety in her chest, and she said the only thought running through her mind. "You wore them?"

This was apparently the wrong thing to say, because it set the women off on a whole new tirade. Finally, Monica noticed the commotion and swooped into the rescue. Mina expected her to go off on the rude woman, like people did in TikTok videos whenever a "Karen" went into a fast-food restaurant and harassed the servers. But Monica didn't. She gave the rude, screaming woman a full refund and took back the bag of used panties.

"What do we do with these?" Mina asked, praying that the answer wasn't going to be put them back out on the floor.

"Cut them up and throw them in the trash," Monica huffed.

"Why do you want me to cut them up first?" Mina asked, confused.

Monica rolled her eyes as if the answer was the most obvious thing in the world. "So that if someone goes digging through the trash, they won't get a free defective Luscious product."

"I don't think it's defective. She said that they shrank in the wash," Mina tried to explain.

"Doesn't matter. Any returned items that can't go back out to the floor for sanitary reasons get cut up and thrown in the trash. Same goes for bras that have pilling, or ripped lace, or broken clasps. Cut. Then trash."

"Okay." Mina nodded as she looked around for a pair of scissors. She felt weird about cutting up a perfectly good piece of clothing — it seemed so wasteful. Even if it had been worn, it was washed at least! She hovered with scissors in her hands, imagining a landfill full of bras and panties. *But what else would we do with them? Donate them? Put them in a sale bin?* She did as she was told because she couldn't think what else could be done with them. She cut each panty into pieces and threw them in the trash as Monica watched her closely. Mina looked down at her toes, feeling like she'd failed again.

Monica sighed. "Why don't you take your fifteen-minute break, and when you get back, we'll figure out what we're going to do with you." Mina nodded and walked back to the staff room. She paused in the doorway, feeling a rush of anxiety. Her heart pounding, she hurried into the employee bathroom and locked the door. She splashed some cold water on her face, closed her eyes, and tried to remember her box breathing technique.

In, two, three, four.

Hold, two, three, four.

Out, two, three, four.

Hold, two, three, four.

In, two, three, four.

Hold, two, three, four.

Out, two, three, four.

Hold, two, three, four.

She put a hand on her chest and tried to imagine her breaths untying the knots twisting inside her. Slowly, her shoulders started to relax, her chest began to feel normal, and she let her eyes flutter open. She looked at herself in the mirror. *I'm okay*, she reminded herself, *everything's okay.*

***

With only five minutes left on her break, Mina rushed out of the bathroom, knocking into Lexie as she rounded the counter to the break room.

"Oh shit! I'm sorry!" Mina stammered.

"Hey!" Lexie laughed. "It's all right, you scared me."

Mina held her breath as the familiar feeling of shame sank into her limbs as it always did following her anxiety attacks.

"Are you okay?" Lexie asked. Mina nodded, trying to keep a neutral face. She was worried that if she told Lexie she was having a bad day, she might start crying. "Did that woman at the cash upset you?"

"You heard that?" Mina looked up at her, embarrassed.

"The people in the food court heard it!" Lexie joked. Mina smiled, laughing in spite of herself. "Don't let people like that get you down. They're not worth it."

"I can't help it." Mina looked down, falling back into the shame spiral.

"Oh," Lexie replied in an understanding tone.

"I'd love to be able to just let it go, but I can't!

My body decides what to freak out about, and it has nothing to do with what is and isn't worth worrying about," Mina rambled. "One time, I got anxious driving in the car with my dad to get ice cream. To get ice cream! We were literally going to my favourite place to get my favourite treat, and the stupid anxiety snake that lives in my chest said, *Hm. Yes. Quite. This seems like an ideal time for a panic attack!*"

Lexie stared at Mina, dumbstruck. Mina's cheeks flushed. *What am I saying?!*

"Does this anxiety snake have a monocle and a top hat? 'Cause you make him sound like someone who would wear a monocle and a top hat." Lexie questioned in a mock-serious tone. They both burst out laughing. "Do you really call it an anxiety snake?"

"I don't know. When I get anxious I always imagine a snake coiling in my chest." Mina giggled.

"That's kind of perfect, actually." Lexie nodded, picturing the snake.

"Thank you." Mina felt herself blushing.

"For what?" Lexie asked, genuinely confused.

"I don't know, but I feel better." Mina sighed. Lexie looked like she was holding back a smile. She awkwardly shifted her weight and rubbed the back of her neck.

"Well, if there's anything else I can do, just let me know." She shrugged and smiled.

"Okay, thanks," Mina said as they passed each other in the hall, their hands touching slightly.

"Actually, why don't I talk to Monica about putting you on the merchandising team?" Lexi asked.

"Do you think I'd be good at it?"

"I don't know, but you won't have to talk to customers."

"Sounds great!" Mina exclaimed, making Lexie laugh again.

"It's a good gig. We collect shipments, push product out onto the floor before the store opens, hang signage, and make sure everything looks good. There is one downside, though," Lexie warned, "shift starts at six a.m."

"I can handle it," Mina said.

"Great, I'll tell my supervisor and see if she can convince Monica to release you to the dark side."

"The dark side? Oh, jeez, now I'm scared," Mina teased.

"Don't worry, I'll protect you. They call me the snake-charmer," Lexie joked. They both started to laugh again. Then Mina started to laugh even harder, gripped her sides, her eyes tearing up. "What?" Lexie asked, chuckling uncomfortably at Mina's reaction.

"I was just thinking," Mina said between gasps, "if we had a line of panties for men, The Snake-Charmer would be a perfect name for them!"

Lexie howled with laughter, practically falling over. She put her hand on Mina's shoulder to steady herself. They looked at one another and burst into another fit of laughter until Monica popped her head in the backroom and reminded Mina that her break was over. Lexie apologized for distracting Mina, wiping away tears of laughter. When Mina returned to the cash, she had a smile on her face that felt like it might stay forever.

05 The Dark Side

MINA'S FATHER OFFERED to drive her into work for her first 6:00 a.m. shift, since he started work around the same time. She was grateful not to have to take the bus. Monica had made a big show about losing her to the merchandising team, but in reality Mina felt like the boss was glad to see her go. She didn't really fit in with the other sales associates. And Monica was constantly watching her, which made Mina feel like she was keeping a running tally of all her mistakes.

Lexie had told Mina to go to the mall entrance on the second floor by parking lot C. The sun was just starting to peek out over the horizon, but still, in the dim light the nearly empty parking lot looked kind of creepy.

"Are you sure this is right?" her father asked.

"I'm pretty sure . . ." she replied, uncertain. She looked around and saw Lexie walking up from the underground parking. "There's Lexie!"

"Lexie, hm?" her dad mumbled.

She leaned across to the driver seat and gave him a quick hug before bouncing out of the car.

"Bye, Dad."

He gave a little wave to her and Lexie, then waited until they were safely inside before driving off.

"Thanks, Aaron," Lexie said as Aaron, the security guard waiting by the door, let them in.

"No problem," he replied, smiling broadly. "You Luscious girls get up early," he teased, cocking his head to the side and eyeing Lexie.

"Early bird gets the worm, didn't you know?" Lexie called over her shoulder.

"I'm more of a night owl," he joked loudly.

Mina kept pace with Lexie and couldn't help but notice her flirtatious relationship with the security guard. He was good-looking, definitely the kind of guy who was used to talking to pretty girls. Clearly they knew each other. *Damn*, she thought. *Wait, what? Damn? Damn what? Why do I care?*

As if she'd heard Mina's inner struggle, Lexie joked, "He flirts with all the girls. Just wait 'til he learns your name." She rolled her eyes playfully.

"Oh," Mina laughed, "guys don't really flirt with me much."

"Or maybe you're just oblivious to it," Lexie said with certainty.

"Maybe." Mia nodded. That could very well be the case. She wasn't exactly the best at reading people. Lexie and Mina walked through the mall to the entrance of Luscious Lingerie, where a small group of other employees were waiting.

"I'm Em," said a tall, thin woman with a casual skater look. "I'm the merchandising supervisor." Mina shook her hand. "This is Madison, Yui, Chase, and obviously you already know Lexie."

Mina waved shyly at them. Everyone was still half asleep but seemed happy to welcome her to the team. Em unlocked the large gate that secured the entrance, and everyone scooted inside. After they logged in and hauled out the boxes of new merchandise to unload, they set themselves up around the panty display table. Madison pulled out her phone and began scrolling for music.

"What do we feel like this morning?" she asked.

"*Rocky Horror?*" Chase suggested as they cut open a box of panties.

"No musicals today, please!" Yui whined.

"Fine," Chase groaned.

Madison shook her head and put on a pop playlist that everyone seemed to enjoy.

Lexie walked Mina through the process: sorting, folding, stacking. Mina stood next to Lexie at a shared pile of panties. She took them one by one, folding and organizing them as Lexie had shown her.

"Did you guys hear about what's going on in the States?" Lexie asked.

"Ugh, guys?" Chase cringed.

"Sorry, thank you! Did you *folks* hear about what's going on in the States?" Lexie corrected herself and then leaned over to Mina and added, "I'm trying to kick the habit of saying *guys.*"

"You're going to have to be more specific," Yui replied.

"Come on, Lex, it's too early for a political rant," Madison said.

"It's never too early!" Lexie laughed manically, making the rest of the group chuckle. She seemed to be the only one who was wide awake. They went on to talk about anti-drag laws being protested, the new models Luscious Lingerie invited to walk in their summer fashion show, Chase's second-year biology course that they were talking over the summer, and Yui's upcoming poetry reading. The group finished up the sorting process as Em returned from the office.

"Alrighty folks, let's get running!" she said as she

picked up a handful of bras. "Lexie, why don't you and Mina pair up?" Mina took a handful of bras and followed Lexie around the store.

"This is the fastest way to learn where everything is," Lexie explained as she led Mina around the store and showed her how to properly stock items. There was a size and colour order to everything. Lexie taught her "ROYGBV," pronounced *roy-gee-biv*, which represented the colours of the rainbow and the order the bras were placed in. Larger sizes were put in the back, and smaller ones in the front so the bigger sizes didn't hide them.

Lexie was right: by the third handful, Mina was starting to get the hang of it. She knew by the style which items belonged in each section of the store, and soon she was zooming around on her own. Between running product to the floor and chatting with the others, she didn't even realize that a couple of hours had passed. She took her last handful of bras into the push-up section and started putting them away. She paused and looked up at the giant poster of one of the

Luscious models hanging above her. Mina couldn't help but suck in her stomach as she passed by and wondered who this woman really was.

Yes, she's beautiful, but there's got to be more to it than that, right? she hoped. When Mina returned to the panty table, the rest of the crew was cleaning up.

"All right, why don't you all go on your fifteen, and I'll pack up the rest of this," Em suggested. Everyone nodded and headed to the break room, where they gathered their wallets and phones; no purses meant no bag check.

"Come grab coffee with us." Madison beckoned to Mina.

"Oh, okay." Mina grabbed her wallet and left the store with the rest of the team. They made their way up to the food court and ordered from the only place open at 8:00 a.m.: Tim Hortons. They all sat around a table in the food court and sipped their coffees.

"So, what's your verdict?" Chase asked Mina.

"On what?" Mina asked.

"Merchandising over sales," they explained.

"Oh, definitely merchandising," Mina blurted out. The group laughed. "I like not having to deal with people."

"Amen to that!" Lexie lifted her coffee cup, and the rest of the group joined her. She gave Mina a wink, which made her blush. They all walked back to the store together, laughing and chatting. When they arrived, other employees had started to clock in, and Mina found that she liked the energy and flurry of preparation; it felt like the opening night of a theatre show and the curtain was about to open.

06 Living Bra Vida Loca

OVER THE NEXT FEW WEEKS, Mina settled into her position on the merchandising team and even made some new friends. She had some hiccups along the way though. Like accidentally attaching a security tag to herself and setting off the alarms. Or showing a guy where he could pick out pyjamas for his wife and lingerie for his mistress. And then there was trying to befriend the mice that lived in the walls — they would scurry across the floor in the early hours when the mall was quiet. Through it all, Lexie was there laughing, helping, and comforting. Whenever Mina started to feel anxious, she would put her hand on her chest and think about Lexie, the snake-charmer, helping her uncoil. Mina noticed that Lexie had started to touch her arm when she wanted Mina's attention and lean in close when Mina talked to her.

Maybe it's nothing or maybe . . . no! Mina wouldn't let herself think about Lexie that way. She wasn't Lexie's type. She just knew it.

Mina had agreed to work a split shift. This meant extra long hours and working in sales to cover someone else's shift when they called in sick. Luscious Lingerie was hosting their annual summer sale, and the store was packed. No one was allowed to book time off during the week of the sale. People had taken to calling in sick instead.

"Oh really?" Monica said over the phone. Mina was working the cash and overheard her conversation. "Well then, you won't mind bringing in a doctor's note, will you?" Monica sneered as she hung up in a huff. Mina wondered if the person on the other end really was sick or if they just wanted to avoid the chaos of the sale. Either way, Monica stomped off to the break room to call every other available employee to come in.

After her shift, Mina hung around and decided to do a little shopping; the sales were too good to beat. She picked out a bra for her mother and one for her sister, and a few things for herself. It was nice to have her own money and spend it how she liked. She was eating out and shopping a little more than she should, but most of her paycheque was going into her savings account for college. On her first payday, she was shocked to discover that minimum wage didn't go very far after all the deductions. So picking up extra shifts was the only way to supplement her spending and meet her savings goals.

Mina returned home with a few shopping bags hanging from her arms and was greeted by a family gathering in the kitchen. Thea Georgia, Cousin Antonia, and Uncle Christos were eating, drinking, and chatting with her parents and siblings. They had opened some champagne and were fussing over her cousin.

"What's going on?" Mina asked as she entered the kitchen.

"Mina, finally, come in!" Her mother ushered her into the tightly packed kitchen. Mina kissed her aunt and uncle on both cheeks and said hi to her cousin.

"We wanted to wait for the whole family to be together, but we couldn't resist — Antonia is engaged!" Thea Georgia exclaimed. Alexandra and her father raised their glasses in congratulations.

"Wow! Congratulations." Mina hugged her cousin. Antonia showed off her ring with false modesty. Her father passed Mina a glass filled with juice and her aunt told her all about the size and cut of the diamond. Her mother had set out a spread of cheese, olives, bread, and fruit to celebrate. Mina reached for a piece of bread, feeling hungry after her long shift, but her mother lightly smacked her hand away and pushed a dish of grapes toward her instead. Resentfully, Mina ate a grape.

"Our Alexandra will be next," Voula said proudly.

Alexandra smiled and took another sip of champagne, finishing the glass.

"So many exciting things happening in the family," Uncle Christos chimed in. "Alexandra's acceptance to medical school, Antonia's engagement, Dimitri's internship, and . . ." He paused as he turned to Mina. Lost for words, he looked her up and down, trying to find some compliment to bestow her with.

"I got a job at the mall . . ." Mina muttered, embarrassed.

"*Yamas!*" her dad shouted, taking the attention off her. Everyone clinked their glasses. "Let's get a picture." They all squeezed in as Yiannis raised his phone for another family selfie to add to his collection. Voula tugged at her shirt and sucked in her stomach, but not before gently tapping Mina's belly and reminding her to do the same.

After the photo, Mina slipped away to her room with that familiar feeling slithering into her stomach and tightening in her chest. She took some deep breaths as she dropped her shopping bags on the floor and flopped onto her bed. *Well*, she thought, *that feels great . . . just great.* A moment later there was a knock at her door, and her dad poked his head inside.

"You okay?" he asked. Mina shrugged, and he sat down on the bed next to her. "Your Uncle Christos didn't mean anything by it. You know he can't keep all his nieces and nephews straight. Half the time he calls you Alexandra." He laughed.

I know, she thought. *That's the problem.*

"Yeah," Mina reassured him, "I'm fine." She was used to being forgotten about when it came to family achievements. There was always someone in her family who was doing bigger and better things. Besides, she hadn't done anything amazing, so what praise would she have deserved anyway?

"Once you start school in the fall, everything will feel back on track," he assured her.

"Right . . ." Mina agreed, but things didn't feel off track. In fact, things felt better than they did when she was in school. She knew her parents had an idea of what success should look like, and their expectations for their children were high — like many immigrant parents, Mina supposed. But if they didn't insist she go to university or college, she probably would have opted to take a year off.

She knew they weren't pleased with her decision to go to community college either. Despite being accepted to several universities — including the school where her sister finished her undergrad — Mina had chosen to go to community college and study Business Tourism. To be honest, she didn't even know exactly what that was, she just knew that she wanted to travel and had to do something to satisfy her parents.

"You know that we're very proud of you, right?" he asked.

She nodded and gave him a reassuring smile. He patted her on the head and went back downstairs.

She lay in bed for a few hours, thinking, questioning her existence and the meaning of life.

Then her phone dinged. A new notification from the work group chat Lexie had added her to — it was just the merchandising team. *At least I have friends*, she thought.

Madison: You all coming over to watch the fashion show this weekend?

Chase: Hellz ya!

Lexie: I'm down!

Yui: Me too!

Lexie: @Mina?

Mina assumed they were talking about the Luscious Lingerie fashion show; it was a big deal. Usually there were a couple celebrities who would walk the runway, fashion icons would fill the audience, and a famous musician would perform. It was kind of like a Super Bowl half-time show, where they'd get a sneak peek of the new product coming to the stores. Mina typed out her reply and hit *Send*.

Mina: I'll be there!

07 The Fashion Show

MINA'S PARENTS LET HER take the car for the evening, despite it being a Saturday night. They preferred to go next door to Thea Georgia's for dinner instead of going out. Mina loved driving and couldn't wait to have her own car. When she pulled into the parking lot of Madison's apartment, she noticed Lexie's car parked nearby. She felt her heart skip a beat and hurried to get inside. Madison buzzed her up, and she took the elevator to the third floor, where Lexie was waiting at the door for her.

"You made it!" she squealed as Mina stepped out of the elevator.

Lexie threw her arms around her and led her into the apartment. There were a bunch of other girls from work there, even some of the sales associates — the nice ones, anyway — like Serena, who waved at Mina when she came in. There were some guys there too, boyfriends, Madison's roommates, and Aaron, the security guard from the mall. Most people were drinking, and for the first time Mina realized that she was probably one of the youngest people there, aside from Lexie. At work everyone seemed like they were the same age to Mina; even their supervisor Em, who was clearly in her thirties, seemed closer in age to Mina while they were at work. But here, Mina noticed a difference.

Lexie dragged her over to the couch and sat down next to her. Madison had the fashion show cued up and ready to go. After a few more people arrived, including Chase and Yui, Madison gathered everyone in the living room to start the show. It was pretty spectacular, Mina had to admit. It felt like they were watching a sports game, cheering when they liked something, booing when they thought the garment was hideous, and laughing about how they were going to avoid Monica, who was no doubt going to try to convince them to blow their entire paycheques on the new inventory.

"Oh god, here we go." Chase rolled their eyes when the announcer showcased their new Pride Collection.

"I don't know, it's kind of nice," Mina argued.

"It's corporate greed and capitalism at its best! I mean, none of the models are queer, the CEO isn't queer, and what the hell has Luscious Lingerie ever done for the LGBTQIA+ community?" Chase rebutted.

"Okay." Mina threw her hands in the air and admitted defeat. "You make a good point."

"Sorry, this stuff really gets to me," Chase said.

"No need to apologize," Mina assured them. "I get it." Chase smiled.

"Hey, look!" Yui pointed to the TV. "They have a panty with the non-binary flag on it!" Chase perked up and watched the model turn on the runway.

"Okay, I do like that," Chase admitted. "But my point still stands!" They all laughed in agreement.

Aaron sat down on Mina's other side after getting up to grab a beer. He cracked it open and took a sip. Some foam dribbled down his chin. Mina stared as he laughed to himself and wiped his chiselled face with a napkin. *Hm,* Mina thought, *he is pretty cute.* Aaron looked at Mina, catching her in the act of staring, and smiled at her. Mina blushed and returned her attention to the TV screen.

"What did I miss?" He leaned over to Mina.

"The lure of corporate pride," Mina replied.

"Oh, so not much," he joked.

"Nope." Mina laughed.

"It's Mina, right?" He extended his hand.

"Yeah." Mina shook his hand, which lingered in hers a little longer than normal.

"Aaron. It's nice to meet you," he said, flashing

her a coy smile and resting his arm on the back of the sofa behind Mina.

"You part of the Pride community?" he asked.

"The Pride community?" Mina laughed. "You mean the queer community? Or the LGBTQIA+ community?"

He scratched the back of his neck. "Yeah, that's what I meant." Mina could feel Lexie leaning toward them, trying to overhear.

Mina nodded. "Yeah, I am. I'm bi." She didn't have too many people asking her about her sexuality. It wasn't anything she tried to hide, but she was pretty straight-passing, and she hadn't really dated anyone. She remembered when she was fourteen, telling her mother that she had feelings for a girl at her summer camp. Her mother had told her that that didn't mean she was gay — some people were just special.

She wasn't entirely wrong, Mina thought. *I'm not gay, I'm bi, and some people are definitely special. It's not like I'm attracted to all men and all women. I'm attracted to non-binary people too. Wait, that's more than two different types of people . . . but "bi" means two. Am I tri? No. Pan? Wait, what?!*

"Hot." Aaron looked her up and down again, which brought her crashing back to reality and reminded her how thankful she was to have options outside of boys. Suddenly he didn't look so cute anymore. Lexie reached across her and smacked Aaron on the chest.

"Don't be gross. Not all bi girls are into threesomes," she scolded. "I know that's what you're thinking."

He shrugged carelessly and stayed close to Mina for the rest of the evening. Madison offered Lexie and Mina a drink, but they both said no. Mina usually didn't like parties, not that she got invited to a lot of them. They usually stressed her out but she was having a great time watching the fashion show, eating chips, and gossiping about other people at work. She and Lexie looked at one another every time something funny happened, and Lexie even rested her hand on Mina's thigh for a moment, which sent chills through her body.

After the fashion show, they all stuck around and hung out. Yui was on her feet telling a hilarious story about how the mice in the store outsmart the exterminators. Mina got up to go to the washroom, and when she came out, Aaron was waiting outside the door.

"Sorry, it's free now," Mina said as she moved aside to let him pass.

"Actually, I was waiting for you." He smiled and leaned against the wall, cornering her.

"Oh, what for?" Mina asked, already knowing the answer.

"It's just so loud in there. I thought maybe we could talk somewhere quiet. Or we could go down to my car," he suggested, leaning in closer.

"Thanks, but I think I'd rather hang out with everyone else."

"What? You don't trust me? I won't do anything if you don't want me to. You don't think I'm that kind of guy, do you?"

"No, I just want to hang out with my friends." She smiled uneasily.

"Aren't we friends?"

"Sure," she said, feeling the panic rise in her chest.

"Then let's hang out." He was so close she could smell the beer on his breath.

"No," Mina replied firmly.

"Why not?"

"Because I don't want to. Now move."

"Jeez." He threw his hands in the air and moved to the side, making a big show of clearing out of her way. Mina held her head high and walked past him and back to the living room.

"Hey, I think I'm gonna head out," she announced to the room. Her friends groaned and tried to convince her to stay longer, but Mina didn't feel like being around people anymore. Lexie gave her a weird look and offered to walk her out. She could tell something was wrong.

When they got down to the parking lot, Mina threw her purse into the car and perched on the hood. Lexie sat next to her. She told Lexie about her interaction with Aaron and how stupid she felt for getting upset over it.

"It's not stupid!" Lexie asserted. "That creep followed you to the bathroom and then cornered you. I'm going to kick his ass when I go back up there. And wait until Madison hears about this!"

"Thank you." Mina sighed.

"No problem. I'll gladly punch him in his stupid face."

"No, not for that! For . . . listening."

"Of course, that wasn't right," Lexie replied. She seemed to settle down a bit, leaning back and looking up at the night sky. "So, other than creepy Aaron coming on to you, did you have a good time?"

"I did. I don't usually like parties, but this was fun. I feel like I need to go on a diet immediately, but other than that, it was really lovely," Mina joked. Sort of.

"Ah, don't get hung up on the whole supermodel thing. Supermodels don't even look like supermodels and besides, you're . . . perfect." Lexie looked away as she said it. Thankfully, because Mina felt herself turning the colour of a ripe tomato. They sat in silence for a moment, neither one sure if they should say what they were both thinking. "I'm bi too. Just so you know."

"Good to know."

"And I'm also off tomorrow," Lexie added.

"Me too."

"Any plans?"

"Nope. You?"

"Nope."

"Cool. Cool, cool, cool." Mina would have smacked herself in the face if she'd thought it would help her speak better. They sat in silence.

"You want to hang out?" Lexie finally asked.

"Yes!" Mina blurted. "Yeah, that would be great."

"Sweet, I'll text you and we'll figure out a time."

"Perfect." Mina smiled.

"I should get back in there. Gotta help Madison violently throw Aaron out on the street or school him in proper human etiquette. I don't know, I'll decide once I'm up there." Lexie laughed as she backed away from Mina's car. "Text me when you get home?"

"I will," Mina said. She watched as Lexie turned on her heel and ran back inside.

Mina's heart pounded with excitement.

08 *Closer*

MINA'S MOTHER SCOLDED HER for sleeping in late, but she couldn't help it. After she'd messaged Lexie to let her know that she got home safely, they spent half the night texting. Lexie told her, in great detail, how Madison and Chase had confronted Aaron after she told them what he did. The other guys at the party reamed him out for his behaviour.

Her mother poured her a cup of coffee as Thea Georgia barged in through the back door.

"How was your party, Mina?" Thea Georgia asked. Mina knew that her mother told Thea Georgia everything and wasn't surprised that she knew about the party.

"It was fine." She decided to leave out the part about Aaron.

"Did you meet any boys there?" her aunt probed.

"None that I liked," Mina replied.

"You should come to the village with your Uncle Christos and I. We'll find you a husband there, a good Greek husband."

"Thanks, Thea, but I think I'll manage without a husband." Mina rolled her eyes playfully. It was pretty typical for her mother and Thea Georgia to ask her about her love life. She never had anything to report, but they always asked. Mina figured it was all with good intentions, but the constant reminder almost forced her to prioritize being in a relationship over other life goals — which she didn't like.

"Or a wife?" her mother chimed.

"Yes, yes, find a wife, not a husband. Much

better," Thea Georgia declared, sipping the coffee Voula placed in front of her.

"I'll get right on that." Mina took her mug of coffee and went back upstairs, leaving her mother and Thea Georgia to chat in the kitchen.

She had come out to her parents a year ago, and it had gone quite well. They had looked to one another with no expression of surprise and said, "Okay, why are you telling us this?"

To which Mina explained that if she ever brought a girlfriend home, she wanted them to be okay with that. They interrogated her about what kind of girlfriend she would be nervous about bringing home to meet them. "Are you in trouble? Did this girl force you to do something you didn't want to do? Why don't you want us to meet her?" Then Mina had to explain that she was speaking hypothetically, and no, she wasn't in any kind of trouble with a girlfriend that she was secretly hiding from them! All in all, it went pretty much as expected.

Mina stared at her closet and started to pull out outfit options. She and Lexie had decided to go for a walk that afternoon. Lexie had suggested going to the beach if the weather was nice, but Mina didn't want her first date with Lexie to be in a bikini. *Date? Is it a date?* She wasn't totally sure. Regardless, she wanted to wear something cute and comfortable.

She tried on a pair of denim shorts that she loved. They made her butt look really great, but they were short . . . and they'd be walking. She tossed them aside. She couldn't risk getting chub-rub and being in pain the whole afternoon. She needed something that came down a little longer so her thighs wouldn't rub together. She pulled out more options and finally settled on a pair of black biker shorts and a loose t-shirt with flowers on it. She matched them with a pair of chunky white sneakers and a small cross-body bag. Admiring her choice in the mirror, she couldn't help but look down at her stomach. She forced herself to look away and pulled the shirt forward so that it hung looser in front of her. *Better.*

Finally ready to go, she realized that she should text Lexie and double-check what time she was coming to pick her up. When she picked up her phone, she noticed a text and two missed calls from Lexie twenty minutes ago.

Lexie: I'm here.

She flew down the stairs in a panic. She shouted to her mother as she swung open the front door, "I'm going out, Ma!"

"Wait! Your friend is here," her mother called from the kitchen. *Oh god*, Mina thought as she walked into the kitchen. Lexie was sitting at the table, sandwiched between her mother and her aunt. "Sit down. Lexie was just telling us about the school play she was in last year." Voula smiled.

"We should probably go," Mina replied.

"But we only just got to talking," Thea Georgia began. "Come sit. Eat. We'll make some food." Her aunt and her mother rose from their seats, but Mina intervened. She took Lexie's hand and practically dragged her away from the kitchen.

"No, thanks! We gotta go!" Mina called over her shoulder.

"It was nice meeting you both!" Lexie exclaimed as she followed Mina out the front door and down the driveway to her car.

"You should have yelled up to me when Mom invited you in," Mina muttered when they got in the car.

"Are you mad at me?" Lexie asked.

"What? No!" Mina exclaimed. "It's just my family can be overbearing, and I didn't want you suffering through the Greek Inquisition."

"Oh, no worries there. I was having a great time." Lexie sighed with relief as she drove out of Mina's subdivision. "You sure you don't want to go to the beach? I brought an extra bathing suit just in case."

"I think I'd rather go for a walk," Mina said, feeling guilty for keeping Lexie from the beach.

"Great! I know an awesome trail," Lexie said excitedly. Mina settled into the passenger seat and tried not to let her brain convince her that Lexie secretly didn't want to be there.

09 Ice Cream

LEXIE AND MINA ARRIVED at the trail. Mina checked out the trail map by the entrance and was thankful that it seemed mostly flat. She'd never been to this trail before and was excited to explore. They walked in silence, the birds fluttering and chirping in the trees. It was nice to be outside. Mina felt like she had spent most of her summer break hunkered down in the mall. She arrived before the sun was up and was too exhausted by mid-afternoon to go out and do anything.

As they approached the first hill on the trail, Mina tried to control her breathing so Lexie wouldn't notice her huffing and puffing the whole way. *Damn, why did I think this was a good idea?* She couldn't help panting as they reach the top. Embarrassed, she glanced over at Lexie, who was also panting.

"Jeez," Lexie exhaled. "I'm so out of shape."

"Me too." Mina laughed. They smiled at one another and took a deep breath. The rest of the walk felt much easier now that they weren't trying to impress one another. They talked and laughed along the trail. They discovered that they had even more in common than they thought; they both enjoyed the *Fast and Furious* movies.

"I just love movies that know what they are and lean into it, you know?" Lexie mused.

"And what they are is action-packed-cheese, right?" Mina clarified.

"No," Lexie answered with mocking expression. "What they are is a *family*," she explained in her best Vin Diesel voice, making Mina croak with laughter.

Their favourite ice cream flavour was chocolate.

"I know it's so typical, but why mess with a good thing, right? Unless you add more chocolate to the chocolate — like hot fudge," Mina explained.

And they both played soccer growing up.

"What position?" Lexie asked

"Keeper," Mina answered. "My dad was a keeper, my brother, and my older sister. We're a family of keepers."

"Impressive. No one wanted to be goalie on the team I played on in junior high, so we had to rotate the position, which sucked! Needless to say, we were the worst team in the league." Lexie laughed.

They walked at an even pace, neither wanting to rush. Mina talked about her family, and going to college, and how, unlike her siblings who'd always known exactly what they wanted to do, she didn't really know what she wanted.

"I kind of feel like a disappointment. My parents do so much for me, and I haven't achieved any of the things they want me to."

"I get that." Lexie sighed. "But sometimes life takes the reins, and you just have to follow wherever it leads. Even if it takes you places you'd rather not be."

"Does your family put a lot of pressure on you too?" Mina asked gently, very aware of Lexie's sudden change in body language. Her shoulders drooped forward and her eyes drifted aimlessly to the ground.

"They don't mean to," Lexie replied, still in her own world. Mina didn't want to pry, but she also felt conflicted about seeing Lexie struggle and not knowing how to help. She decided she would wait and let Lexie open up when she was ready.

"I'm always here, if you want to talk about it," she offered. Lexie gave an absentminded nod in reply.

When they reached the end of the trail, which looped back around to the parking lot, there was an ice cream truck opening up. More couples and families had arrived to walk the trail and spend the day outside.

Lexie grinned at Mina, eyeing the ice cream truck. She was finally shaken out of her daze. They got ice cream, chocolate of course, and sat at a nearby picnic table enjoying their chilly treat. After they finished, Lexie drove Mina home and lingered in the driveway to say goodbye.

"Thanks for the date," Lexie muttered, blushing.

Mina felt her stomach flip. "So it was a date?" she asked, a smile creeping across her face.

Lexie nodded. "I'd like it if it was."

"Me too," said Mina.

Lexie reached across to the passenger seat and gently pulled Mina's face toward her. She kissed her softly on the cheek. Mina felt herself flush and bit her lip to keep from smiling too big.

"I'll see you later?" Lexie asked.

"Definitely," Mina replied. She hopped out of the car and waved to Lexie, who took off down the street. Mina felt like she could jump up onto the roof with this new energy coursing through her. *Lexie likes me. Lexie. The coolest, prettiest, most fearless person I've ever met likes me!* Lexie was the first person that Mina ever felt this way about. Okay, she did have a crush on Dylan McNeil in junior high, but he didn't count. He was an irresistible Harry Styles type, but Lexie was WOW. She was Lexie.

Mina's father was in the kitchen cooking dinner while her mother did a crossword puzzle at the kitchen table.

"Somebody had a good time," her mother pried, but Mina didn't care. She was too happy.

"What did you do today?" her father asked.

Mina took a deep breath before she replied. "I went on a date."

"So it *was* a date!" her mother exclaimed. "I knew that girl was a lesbian because of the plaid shirt."

"Ma! You can't tell if someone's gay by what they're wearing!"

"Are you gay now? I thought you were high-sexual," her father asked, confused.

"Bisexual, Dad, well actually it's pansexual I think. Didn't you read the pamphlets I brought home from Pride last year?"

"So are you and Lexie girlfriend and girlfriend now?" her mother questioned.

"Uh, no, not yet. It was just our first date," Mina stammered.

"Oh." Her mother sighed, disappointed. She gave Mina a once over, eyeing her outfit. "Is that what people wear on dates now?"

"What's wrong with it?" Mina asked.

"Nothing," her father intervened. "You look lovely."

"She looks pregnant," Voula replied. Mina stood in stunned silence for a moment before pulling at her shirt.

"Voula —" her father started, but her mother cut him off.

"What? Am I not allowed to say what I think?" She shrugged in genuine confusion.

"Mom, you can't just say stuff like that," Mina argued.

"Wouldn't you rather know that the shirt makes you look big?" Voula countered.

"No," Mina replied, frustrated. "I like this shirt. It's comfortable. And cute!"

"Oh, Mina, how do you ever expect to get a boyfriend wearing things like that?" Her mother sighed.

"I don't want a boyfriend." Mina folded her arms, standing her ground.

"So you *are* gay?" her father interjected.

"No!" Mina answered.

"A girlfriend then," Voula said, throwing her hands in the air as if Mina was being the unreasonable one.

"I just mean that I don't want a partner who only cares about how I look! I want to date someone who likes me for me," Mina exclaimed.

"Yes, I want that for you too. Did I say that I didn't want that for you?" her mother said. "But if you were . . . *healthier*, more boys, or girls, whatever, would find you attractive. That's just how it is."

"If I was thinner, you mean," Mina snapped.

"I didn't say that. Did you hear me say that?"

"I don't want you to comment on my body."

There was a moment of intense silence. "I'm just telling you my opinion," Voula said.

"Well, I didn't ask for it," Mina replied.

"Fine, wear whatever you want. Don't listen to me."

"Now, now," her father intervened again. "Maybe no one says anything about how we look. Okay?" Mina nodded, and Voula leaned back in her chair with her arms folded over her chest. "Maybe we could all go out for family walks in the evening? Wouldn't that be nice? Exercise and spend some quality time together."

Mina stared, shocked and deeply hurt by her father's attempt to "help." Tears welled in her eyes as she turned on her heel and ran to her room.

"Mina!" he called after her, but she didn't turn around.

***

A perfect day ruined. Mina's mother was always fussing about her weight. Ever since she was a kid, her mother used to say that she was "big boned" — whatever that means — and assure her that she would lose her "baby weight" when she was older. Much to Voula's disappointment, Mina never did. Voula would praise

Mina's older sister for being trim, fit, and beautiful, while Mina got the disappointed sighs and criticism. Mina had almost become numb to it. Almost.

She slammed her bedroom door and locked it. Then stood in front of her mirror and looked at herself. She was fully crying now. That familiar feeling of the anxiety snake coiling in her chest was settling in for a long stay.

Mina went down for dinner when she was called later that evening but didn't speak to her mother. Voula seemed to be carrying on as usual, obviously convinced Mina would get over their little spat. They had fought about her weight before, but this time it felt different. Like her deepest fear, the thing she always worried people were thinking about her, was actually true. She was broken and unlovable. Her date with Lexie was far from her mind now. Her father watched her cautiously all through dinner but didn't say anything for fear of making things worse. Her siblings carried on talking about their day and asking about news of their cousin's wedding.

Deflated and exhausted, Mina excused herself right after dinner and dragged herself back upstairs. She wanted to be alone. She sat at her desk and flipped through Instagram. @LusciousLingerie had a new post featuring one of the models from their fashion show at the beach in a new bikini, her long legs kicking playfully at the clear blue waters. Mina sighed and was about to throw her phone across the room when a text from Lexie appeared. Just in the nick of time.

Lexie: Had a great time today :) Excited to see you at work tomorrow.

Mina: Me too.

Mina smiled briefly and a spark of hope flared in her stomach.

10 Luscious Love

THE NEXT WEEK working at Luscious Lingerie went by in a flash. Mina was happy to be spending time away from home. Away from her mother. Mina was really getting into the flow of stocking and loving the team she was working with. They would go to the movies, grab coffees on their early shifts, and message each other constantly over the group chat. They made the early morning shifts, the minimum-wage pay, and the near-body-dysmorphia bearable.

There were still lots of stressful moments, like when Mina caught someone shoplifting, or when she had to dispose of a used tampon from the dressing room, or when Monica yelled at her for showing up fifteen minutes late because she missed the bus. But through it all, Lexie and the team were there. Mina especially liked spending time with Lexie.

Madison, Chase, Yui, Lexie, and Mina sat in the food court on their fifteen-minute break, sipping their Tim Hortons Iced Capps and chatting. Aaron approached the table sheepishly, with his thumbs tucked into the belt loops of his security uniform.

"Hey." He waved. No one responded. He looked at Mina. "I'm really sorry about what happened. I was drunk, and I should have backed off."

"Thanks." Mina smiled.

"I'm really not a bad guy," he tried to explain. "Maybe I could take you out sometime, and we could get to know each other?" His earnest attempt to smooth things over wasn't lost on Mina, but she really didn't want to go out with him.

"I'm actually seeing someone, so —"

"Is it serious?" He jumped on her statement.

"Umm . . ." Mina didn't know how to answer, but luckily she didn't have to.

"It is. We're very happy. Thanks," Lexie said, putting her arm around Mina. Aaron looked dumbstruck and backed away, giving an awkward wave to the group.

"So it's official now?" Yui asked, barely containing her excitement. Mina and Lexie made eye contact, communicating without words, and nodded simultaneously. Madison, Chase, and Yui exploded with joy.

"I knew all along," Madison confessed.

"Everyone knew," Chase interjected. "Sorry, but you two weren't subtle about it." Mina and Lexie interlaced their fingers and smiled at each other.

Later that night, Lexie took Mina on a drive out of the city along a scenic route. They stopped for coffees along the way and ended up at a beach. Lexie pulled out a blanket, which she laid out on the sand in front of her car. She invited Mina to lie down beside her and look up at the stars.

"You have to get outside the city to see a night sky like this," Lexie explained. She was right. The stars twinkled and glistened in the clear dark-blue heavens. She pointed out some of the constellations that she knew and showed Mina how to tell the difference between a star and a planet.

"Do you come here often?" Mina asked.

"We're already dating. You don't have to use cheesy pickup lines on me anymore," Lexie joked.

Mina laughed and shook her head. "You know what I mean!"

"Yeah, I do. My mom used to take me here. Sometimes when I'm feeling overwhelmed I come here and look at the stars. They remind me that there's a much bigger universe out there, and somehow that makes me feel like my earthling problems are manageable."

She tried to play it off like a joke, but Mina could tell that she was being very thoughtful and meant it seriously. She reached down and took Lexie's hand.

"Thanks for sharing it with me." Mina turned to face her. Lexie smiled and leaned in, their noses touching. Mina closed her eyes and leaned in the rest of the way until their lips met. Mina felt like fireworks were going off inside her stomach, like fire surged through her limbs. She leaned in again, and Lexie pulled her closer, unable to tear her lips away. When they stopped kissing, Mina could tell that the same energy she felt was coursing through Lexie.

Lexie sat up, all smiles, and winked at Mina as she got to her feet. "You know how to swim?" she asked.

"Uh, yeah, why?" Mina answered. Lexie just continued to smile as she took off her shoes, then her pants, and her top, until she was in nothing but her underwear.

"Let's go for a swim." She giggled with excitement as she ran off toward the water. Mina sat straight up and watched as Lexie headed for the lapping waves. Shrieking, Lexie ran into the water, splashing and laughing.

"Come on, Mina! It's refreshing!" Lexie shouted. Mina sat frozen on the blanket. Her mother's words ran through her mind and the fireworks in her stomach dissolved into nerves. She'd never been in a bikini around someone she liked, let alone her underwear. Sensing that something wasn't right, Lexie jogged out of the water and sat back down on the blanket. Mina could feel the cool water misting off her skin in the warm, humid air. "What's wrong?"

"I just . . . I don't know if I want you to see me . . ." Mina muttered.

"Okay. Why not?" Lexie asked, gently.

"I just . . . I don't know." Mina pulled her knees into her chest and buried her face in her hands.

"Okay. You don't have to tell me." Lexie put her cold, wet arm around Mina's shoulder, and Mina leaned into her embrace. "But just so you know, I already see you. You're beautiful and amazing."

Mina let a burst of laughter escape her lips.

"No, seriously! I'm not just saying that to get you to take your clothes off or anything like that. I think you're beautiful."

Mina felt tears welling up. "Even though I'm not

. . . I mean, you could be dating someone way more attractive than me," she stammered, feeling all her anxieties rush into her body at once.

"And you could be dating someone way more attractive than me," Lexie said without hesitating.

"No! You're . . . I mean, I like you." Mina blurted out. Lexie laughed.

"That's how I feel too."

"It's just . . ." Mina stopped herself.

"What is it?" Lexie asked, full of concern.

Mina sighed. She kept her eyes down, digging her toes deeper and deeper into the sand as she told Lexie about the fight with her mother last week. She told Lexie about her constant nagging insecurities and how hard she tried to be a confident person. She wanted to be a body-positive person, a feminist who appreciated her body's sacredness, but she constantly felt beat down from something or other. Hell, sometimes she just felt too tired to fight back against her negative self-talk. All throughout her explanation, Lexie listened quietly, never interrupting or trying to feed her the typical

"You're not fat, you're beautiful" response Mina so often got when she opened up about her feelings. Like being fat and beautiful were mutually exclusive.

"Wow," was Lexie's response. Mina was convinced that she'd blown it — she'd overshared, and now Lexie wouldn't want to date her after finding out what a mess she really was. "I never knew you were feeling all that. You . . . you seem so together."

"What?" Mina practically shouted.

"I mean, you're going to study business tourism despite what your parents think, you're saving money to pay for the courses yourself — which is hella responsible — and every time shit hits the fan at work you're still one of the kindest people I've ever met." Lexie pulled her in closer. "I'm so sorry your mother said those things to you. That was just wrong."

"Yeah . . ." Mina choked back tears, but it was no use. They streamed down her face.

"You don't have to put so much pressure on yourself. It's impossible to love your body every day. I think just being able to accept your body as is, is hard enough." Lexie put her arm around Mina's waist and let her hand rest on her belly. Mina felt the impulse to swat her hand away or shift her position so that Lexie didn't have to touch her stomach, but Lexie clung tighter to Mina and covered her cheek and neck with kisses. Mina couldn't help but smile and laugh as the kisses tickled her.

She felt very seen, fully clothed and wrapped in Lexie's arms. It felt like she was baring her soul to the night sky. Lexie planted one last kiss on her forehead. "Come on, let's finish our coffees in the car." She stood and helped Mina up.

"Wait," Mina said. She took off her shoes, her shorts, her top. She stood in front of Lexie with her belly curving over the top of her underwear, her cellulite and stretch marks glistening in the moonlight, and her thighs jiggling as she shifted her weight, uncertain. Lexie smiled at her. She relaxed her arms and stood in front of Mina, mirroring her body language. Mina looked at her in awe. She was gorgeous, with perfectly smooth skin, curved in the right places. Lexie was looking back at her with the same expression.

"I know," Lexie said sheepishly, tucking her hair behind her ears. "My arms are super weird."

"What?" Mina responded, looking at Lexie's perfectly normal arms. "What's weird about them?"

Lexie sighed and lifted them out to the sides, making a *T* shape. Mina continued to look for the imperfection that Lexie was talking about but couldn't find anything out of the ordinary.

"Seriously?" Lexie asked in disbelief. "They're freakishly long." Mina looked again, but all she saw was beauty. Mina shrugged and shook her head, indicating that she didn't see it all. Lexie laughed. "I guess we all have a thing about ourselves that no one but us notices."

"I think you're right." Mina nodded, a little disappointed. She couldn't help but think that having longish arms wasn't exactly the same as being fat and didn't quite carry the same stigma, but she didn't say anything. Instead, she reached out to take Lexie's hand. "Shall we go for a dip?"

"Actually, I was lying when I said it was refreshing. It's freakin' cold." Lexie shivered.

Mina laughed. "Let's get dressed and warm up in the car."

Lexie nodded and gathered her clothes. They sat talking in the car for another hour before deciding it was finally time to go home.

11 Customer Service

MINA SAT WITH LEXIE, Em, and Chase in the break room, eating lunch. Chase was scrolling through their phone while Lexie told Mina a story about nearly falling off the stage in their school's production of *Little Women*.

"I came this close." Lexie held her thumb and her index finger very close together, and Mina laughed. She imagined that, had she been there in the audience, she would have been terrified for Lexie. But hearing it now, the way she told the story, it was hilarious.

Monica burst through the office door, sullen and whiney.

"Ugh, Serena and Taylor called in sick. Does anyone want to pick up an extra shift today?" She looked directly at Mina, knowing full well that Mina would cave. Lexie kicked her under the table. Em didn't look up from her meal, talking while she chewed.

"I can spare someone from my team. We're nearly done," Em mumbled.

Monica's eyes drifted to Mina once again.

"Sure," Mina agreed with a sigh.

"You're my saviour!" Monica sang and rushed back into the office to adjust the schedule. *Funny how Monica never talks to me unless she needs something*, Mina thought. Lexie gave her a look that seemed to say *I tried* and shrugged. They continued eating, and not long after, Mina followed Monica out on to the floor.

"Okay, you remember our training. If they've got a bra in their hands, you show them the matching panty. And make sure they take a second bra into the fitting room with them. We want to encourage our customers to leave with multiple bras," Monica reiterated.

"Right, I remember." Mina nodded along. *I remember why I hate sales.*

"Who knows, maybe if this works out we could get you off the merch team and back into the sales family," Monica added excitedly.

Mina smiled through her dread; that was not her ideal situation, but she wasn't worried. Em liked having her on the team, and she knew that. Unlike the last time Mina worked sales, she was confident in her knowledge about the products. She knew where everything was, which bras fit which breast shapes, and what options there were for colours and sizes. It was much easier this time around, and Mina found herself enjoying the interactions with customers.

"Oh, thank god." A woman sighed, exasperated, as she marched over to Mina. "Finally, a normal-looking person." Mina was confused at first but greeted the customer all the same. "Can you help me find a bra that fits? You know how it is for us bigger girls." The woman took Mina's hand.

"Oh, yes, of course."

"I'm just so happy to see someone working here who looks like me. I literally walked around the whole store, and all I saw was model, model, model, and I started to think maybe I should just leave."

"I'm sure one of the other sales associates would have been happy to help you too."

"Maybe, but I feel more comfortable shopping with someone who's a similar size."

"Fair enough." Mina nodded. "So what are you looking for?"

Shopping for undergarments can be a stressful thing, and Mina understood what it felt like to walk into a place and feel like you didn't belong. She took the woman around the store, helped her in the fitting room, and ended up having a very fun afternoon hunting for the right bra. Monica came to check on her while the customer was in the fitting room trying on the bra they both hoped would be the perfect fit.

"How's it going?" Monica inquired.

"Great! I measured and picked out a great bra for a customer. She's trying it on now," Mina explained joyfully.

"Just the one bra?" Monica raised an eyebrow. "Did you bring her the matching panty at least?"

Mina shook her head. "She didn't want any panties."

Monica rolled her eyes and went back out to the floor. She picked out a few panties and brought them into the dressing room. Without even acknowledging Mina, she knocked on the customer's fitting room door.

"I don't know," the woman inside the dressing room answered. "I think it's too small. Is this the largest size you have?" She opened the door and was surprised to see Monica standing there with a handful of underwear and an insincere smile.

"I thought you might like to try the matching panties," Monica chirped.

"Oh, no thank you," the woman replied, wary of Monica's sudden presence. "Mina —" she started, but Monica cut her off before Mina could answer.

"Did you say you thought this bra was too small?" Monica inspected the fit. "It looks too big to me."

"Really? It's kind of digging in, actually —" the woman tried to explain, but Monica rolled her eyes and cut her off again.

"Mina's still learning how to do fittings. Let me take a look" Monica stepped into the dressing room and closed the door behind her, leaving Mina alone outside.

Mina waited outside the fitting rooms, pretending to fold panties. Finally the customer she had been helping marched out of the fitting rooms in a huff. She didn't even look at Mina as she stormed past her and out of the store. Monica sauntered out shortly after and stood next to Mina, watching the woman disappear into the mall.

"She was really rude. Some people can't be helped." Monica sighed.

"I was helping her," Mina replied through gritted teeth. Monica just shrugged and walked off to the office. Mina bit her tongue and wondered helplessly what Monica had said to upset the customer so much.

At the end of her very long shift, Monica called Mina into the office.

"I was so impressed with the work you did today," she gushed, much to Mina's surprise. Although she noticed that the insincere smile had returned.

"Thank you," Mina replied suspiciously. "I guess this would be a good time to ask for a raise, huh?"

Monica laughed, throwing her head back, then becoming immediately serious.

"No. I was actually going to suggest that you consider participating in the Luscious Lingerie Photo Contest." She handed Mina a freshly printed flyer. "It's a company-wide employee photo contest featuring the 'Real Women' of Luscious Lingerie. They just announced it today. The winner gets one thousand dollars and their photo will be used in marketing material online and in the store. Plus, if you get picked, the store where the employee works wins bonuses for their staff. Stores all over the country are participating. What do you say?"

Mina stared at the flyer in her hands. "Maybe some of the other girls would be interested. Lexie's actually done some modelling —"

"But I want *you* to do it," Monica interrupted.

"Why me?"

"Because you're perfect for this. I think you're a great example of the kind of employee Luscious Lingerie wants to showcase in our stores. I mean, look at what you did today. You can basically work in any department."

Mina wasn't convinced, but it *was* an exciting opportunity. "I'll think about it," she said.

"Excellent! Let me know when you want to take the photo to submit, and we can do it in the store!" Monica opened the office door and let Mina step out into the break room. She gathered her things and stopped to say hi to Madison and Yui, who were in for a night shift. She couldn't help but tell them about the photo contest and how Monica had asked her to participate.

"That's cool," Yui replied.

"Since when do they want 'Real Women'? Plus, you get paid? Ohhhh, do you think it's because of the fashion show backlash?" Madison wondered.

"The what?" Mina asked.

"The store's been getting a lot of flak on social media for only hiring young, thin white models and employees, so the company wants to show how 'woke' they are. They asked Tia to do that too, didn't they?" Yui asked. Mina had worked with Tia a few times. She was a plus-sized Indian woman on the sales team with an amazing laugh and a sleeve of tattoos that Monica made her cover up. *So they only want me because I'm fat*, Mina thought. Being used for her body didn't feel good.

Later that evening, Mina texted Lexie and told her everything that happened at work that day.

Lexie: That's amazing! You should totally do it!

Mina: You think? It feels kinda icky.

Lexie: Sure, they might be doing it for the wrong reasons, but having your face out there in an international marketing campaign would be cool! I mean come on! Plus you'd be making a statement to millions of women that all bodies are beautiful.

Mina: I dunno. I don't like being in the spotlight.

Lexie: You could also read the hell out of Luscious Lingerie after. Talk for real about their lack of diversity on a massive platform.

Lexie: Unless they make you sign an NDA.

Mina: It feels weird to me.

Lexie: But I guess at that point you could call a lawyer in.

Mina: Are you listening to me?

Lexie: Yeah. Are you listening to me?

Mina: I'm not going to do it.

Lexie: You're kidding me. Why not?

Mina: I told you! It doesn't feel right and I don't want to be in the spotlight.

Lexie: Because you're insecure?

Mina: No.

Mina: Not just because of that.

Lexie: You can't let negative self-talk hold you back from doing things that matter.

Mina: I had a feeling you wouldn't understand.

Lexie: What do you mean? I get it, it's complicated. But I still think you should do it.

Mina: No, you don't get it! Being insecure about how long your arms are isn't the same as being fat.

Lexie: Okay, you're kind of downplaying my own insecurity, but sure, I guess it's different. I wish you wouldn't call yourself fat.

Mina: Fat isn't a bad word. I don't know when we started using it as an insult but it's just the way I am and it's not a bad thing! My whole life everyone has wanted me to be different than I am. Better. And now that it's trendy I'm just supposed to forget all that and embrace it? The people at Luscious Lingerie have no idea how much they hurt people. How much they've hurt me.

Lexie: I don't know what to say . . .

Mina: Don't say anything. I need some time alone.

Mina turned off her phone and threw it down on the bed. She stared at the empty black screen. Everything she said was swirling around inside her head, and the walls she built to block out and ignore the toll this job was having on her were finally starting to crumble.

12 Olive Oil and Water

MINA SAT SILENTLY at dinner that night. She didn't dare tell her parents about the contest at work. She was worried that they'd agree with Lexie and somehow force her to do it.

"Mina?" her father questioned. Mina looked up and saw the whole table looking back at her.

"What?" she asked, totally consumed by her thoughts.

"Your mother asked you when you're going to invite Lexie over for dinner."

"Oh, I don't know." Mina shrugged. She and her mother weren't exactly on speaking terms. That is, Mina wasn't speaking to her, but Voula carried on as if nothing was wrong.

"We'd all like to meet her," he encouraged.

"Unless she doesn't exist," Dimitri teased.

"She's real, I met her." Her mother jumped to her defence. "But only the one time, so she'll have to come over again soon and try my baklava."

"Sure," Mina replied, eager to end the conversation.

"When?" her father asked.

"Not tomorrow. I'm going dancing with Thea Georgia," her mother said.

"And Saturday night I have a soccer game," her father chimed in.

"So Sunday?" Alexandra asked.

"Sunday, yes, is she free on Sunday?" her mother probed.

"Do we all have to be there?" Dimitri whined.

"Yes, if Lexie is free on Sunday," Yiannis replied.

"Do you know if she's free?" Voula turned to Mina.

"I don't know!" Mina burst out. The table went silent. She left her plate of food and ran back up to her room. Anxiety coiling in her chest, she lay down on her bed and did her box breathing, but it was too late. She was having an anxiety attack. It didn't matter what she did now — she would have to ride it out. Tears started streaming down her face, her heart was pounding, and she felt like she was being pulled in every direction.

Not long after the attack started, her dad came up to check on her. He knew that when this happened and she was safe at home, the best thing to do was to leave her be until the storm passed. A little while later, he knocked on her door again, poking his head in with a cup of hot tea in hand.

"How are you feeling?" he asked.

"Better, thanks." Mina sat up in bed and took the tea.

"I'm sorry we pushed you to invite Lexie to dinner. You can introduce us when you're ready. There's no rush."

"No, it's not that. I want you to meet her," Mina assured him. "I've just had a lot on my mind lately, and we got into a bit of a fight earlier."

"I see," he replied. "Have you apologized?"

Mina shook her head. "What makes you think I should be the one to apologize? You don't even know what the fight was about!"

"I'm not suggesting you apologize. I just know that you tend to apologize unnecessarily," he explained.

"Sounds like someone else I know." Mina raised her eyebrows at him. Mina's father avoided conflict more than anyone she knew, aside from herself. He could end an argument before it even began. He laughed at her observation.

"If your mother wasn't so skilled at winning arguments, I would suggest we fight more." He chuckled.

"You?" Mina challenged him.

"The occasional argument just means you're invested in the relationship. It means you care about someone enough to try to work through hard times or uncomfortable situations."

"Well, when you put it like that, it doesn't sound so bad." Mina shrugged.

"It's not the end. I hope Lexie isn't the kind of partner who likes to stay angry," he added, cautioning her in the most fatherly way he knew how.

"Me too," Mina agreed.

"If you need anything, you come talk to me, all right?" He patted her on the shoulder and lingered for a moment, seeming to marvel at how grown-up his youngest daughter looked all of a sudden.

It was all too much. Maybe the 6:00 a.m. shifts were finally getting to her. That was it. She probably just needed some sleep. She curled up in bed and turned her phone back on. A flurry of texts and missed calls from Lexie flashed across her screen.

Lexie: Shit. I'm sorry. I shouldn't be pushing you to do this. And you're right. I don't get it. But I'm willing to learn and listen if you'll help me understand?

Lexie: I'm sorry.

Lexie: Mina?

Lexie: Can I call you?

MISSED CALL FROM LEXIE

Lexie: Are you mad?

MISSED CALL FROM LEXIE

Lexie: Fine. Text me when you want to talk.

Mina felt bad about giving her the silent treatment and texted her back with an apology and an explanation.

Mina: Hey. I'm sorry, I turned my phone off. I just needed some time to think about things. I didn't mean to make you worry. You're probably asleep now, so let's chat tomorrow.

Lexie immediately called after she received Mina's text, and Mina's anxiety and anger melted in a flurry of apologies and promises. Lexie was on her side, and having a friend in all this felt good. Feeling confident in their relationship once again, Mina popped the question, "Will you come over for dinner this Sunday and meet my family?"

Lexie excitedly agreed.

***

On Sunday evening, Lexie arrived at Mina's house at 5:30 p.m. on the dot. Mina suspected she'd gotten there early and sat in her car until that exact moment. She had worn a very pretty floral dress, curled her hair, and done her makeup. Mina wasn't used to seeing her all dolled up; usually the 6:00 a.m. shifts were a less glamorous affair. Lexie kissed her on the cheek, and Mina brought her inside. Mina's parents greeted Lexie excitedly and welcomed her in. Mina introduced her to the rest of the family, which included Thea Georgia, Theo Christos, and Cousin Antonia, whom her mother had invited. Her parents made a huge meal: pastitsio, Greek salad, dolmades, moussaka, potatoes, feta and olives, fresh bread, and baklava for dessert. They all dug into the delicious feast.

"Will you act again?" her mother asked Lexie as she passed the potatoes to Alexandra.

"I hope so," Lexie replied. "There are a couple community theatres auditioning for stuff in the fall, so I might submit."

"How exciting," Voula gushed. "We will come to see the play when it's ready."

"What if she gets cast as tree number one, Ma?" Dimitri teased, and Mina kicked him under the table.

"We'll still go. Tree number one is a better part than tree number two." Voula looked to Lexie with a smile, and Lexie laughed appreciatively.

"Is that what you want to do for a career?" Mina's father asked. Mina was surprised by his serious tone.

"No, not for a career. I've always liked programming, so I'm thinking I'll get into computer science eventually," Lexie replied as Mina's mother scooped another helping of pastitsio onto her plate without asking if she wanted more.

"Computer science? I work in IT," her father replied, the strict what-are-your-intentions-with-my-daughter facade melting away as quickly as it had appeared. Much to Mina's delight, they seemed to get along pretty well. He told her all about a new project he was working on. Most of it didn't make sense to Mina, but Lexie seemed interested and able to keep up. "What school will you be attending in September? Somewhere nearby, I hope," he said.

Lexie paused, chewing slowly, before answering. "I'm not going to school in September."

"Oh," Mina's dad remarked, clearly taken aback. The table went silent.

"A gap year is a great opportunity," Mina interjected.

"You'll work and save money for school the next year," Mina's mother replied. "It's good, very good."

"Ahh, no. I'm not sure when I'll get around to university. If ever," Lexie confessed.

"How do you plan on working in the tech industry without an education?" Mina's father questioned.

"Did you go to university?" Lexie asked him.

"No," he replied, a bit annoyed. Mina saw her brother's eyeballs bouncing between their father and Lexie like a tennis ball. The room was tense.

"Well then, why couldn't I work my way into it, like you did?" Lexie stated, straddling the line between stirring up drama and defending herself.

Yiannis thought about it for what felt like an eternity, then nodded and took a sip of his wine. "Well, I suppose, you could." He chuckled, clearly impressed by her confidence.

"Lexie, did you try my moussaka?" Voula interjected, changing the subject entirely and saving them from another awkward silence. She passed the dish of moussaka down the table, and Lexie happily indulged in more food. The rest of the evening rolled on without a hitch. Lexie and her father continued to talk about the tech industry, Lexie gushed over Voula's delicious baklava, and she even made Theo Christos and Dimitri laugh.

At the end of the evening, Mina walked Lexie to her car and thanked her again for coming over.

"Sorry about my dad," Mina said.

"I think he's pretty cool," Lexie said, taking Mina's hand. "Your parents seem like great people."

"They didn't have much when they came from Greece, and they worked really hard to build a better life here. They're all about education, good jobs, and marrying us off to rich spouses who can look after us when they're gone," Mina joked.

"Right," Lexie said thoughtfully.

"I guess when I meet your parents, you'll be overthinking everything too." Mina kissed her cheek, and Lexie smiled. "I'll see you at work tomorrow." Mina waved goodbye and watched as Lexie got in the car and drove away. When she went back inside, she was greeted by a flurry of excitement from her family. They all seemed to approve of Lexie and, to Mina's intense relief, liked her almost as much as Mina did.

13 A Gut Feeling

THE NEXT DAY, Mina got to work at six. The rest of the merch team was waiting outside Luscious Lingerie for her.

"All right," Em said with as much vigour as she could muster so early in the morning, "let's head in."

"Shouldn't we wait for Lexie?" Mina asked.

"She called in sick," Em explained as she unlocked the gates in front of the store. Mina felt a pang of worry in her stomach. The anxiety snake crept slowly into her mind and whispered, *Maybe she's avoiding you*. Mina sighed and shook her head, dismissing the thought quickly. She pulled out her phone and texted Lexie before her shift started.

Mina: Heard you're not feeling well. Hope you're better soon xo.

Mina knew it was silly to worry about a thing like that. Lexie would reply and assure her everything was fine, then they would make plans to hang out once she felt better.

Unfortunately for Mina, that wasn't the case. Lexie called in sick the next day, and the day after that, and the day after that. She also never replied to Mina's texts, and when Mina called to make sure everything was okay, Lexie only talked to her for a minute before telling her she needed to go. With each day that passed, the anxiety snake hissed louder and louder in her ear: *This is because of you. Meeting your family freaked her out! She doesn't like you anymore.*

Mina continued to text and call, reminding Lexie that she was there to help. Em didn't seem to mind having Lexie out sick. If she knew the reason for her absence, she didn't say so. But Monica was definitely annoyed by it.

"This girl, Trish, she used to work here, and in the middle of our Annual Sale, she tried to call in sick because we wouldn't give her the weekend off. The weekend of our biggest sale! I mean, come on. What did she expect me to do?"

"Wasn't her sister getting married?" Em asked. They were all sitting in the break room enjoying their lunch until Monica stormed through with a long list of complaints and woes.

"Um, hello, we're her family too. What about her Luscious sisters who needed her to be here? Besides, I only asked her to work the morning shift. She would have made it on time for the ceremony and all that." Monica rolled her eyes.

Mina ate her yogurt in silence, half listening, half thinking. She was worried about Lexie, but that wasn't the only thing weighing on her mind. Without Lexie's constant distraction and chipper demeanour pulling

Mina through the day, she was starting to lose her rose-coloured glasses. Luscious Lingerie's ugly truth was becoming harder and harder to ignore. Now she was starting to see it for what it really was: a cog in the capitalist machine, preying on women's insecurities and pushing the belief that thin, white, and pretty were the epitome of beauty.

Serena, whom Mina hadn't really talked to since the party, sat down next to her and unpacked her lunch. "Hey Mina!" She smiled. "How are you?"

"Fine, how are you?" Mina snapped out of her daze.

"Oh, you know, livin' the dream. Where's Lexie? I feel like I never see one of you without the other." She chuckled.

"Uh, she's not feeling well."

"Oh no, what's wrong?"

"I don't know." Mina must have looked sullen and upset because Serena immediately leaned forward and patted her hand.

"Oh well, summer is coming to an end," she said knowingly.

"What does that mean?" Mina replied, confused.

"Nothing. I just thought maybe you two were having a fun summer fling, and now you're wrapping things up. You're starting college in the fall, right?" Serena shrugged.

Mina's mind started racing. *A fling? Oh god. Was this just a summer fling? Maybe this relationship means more to me than it does to Lexie, and she really is avoiding me!*

Mina spent the rest of her shift on the edge of a panic attack. She couldn't stop herself from replaying every moment they'd spent together in the last few weeks. She wondered why Lexie would agree to meet her family if she was going to break up with her. After going back and forth, *she loves me, she loves me not*, Mina decided to check in and go to Lexie's house. Em gave Mina Lexie's address. She knew she wasn't supposed to, but she was also getting worried about Lexie, so she felt like a minor breach of privacy was worth making sure her friend was okay.

When Mina got home from work, she went straight to the kitchen, and firmly refusing her mother's help, whipped up a batch of chicken soup. Then she borrowed her parents' car and headed over to Lexie's. She knew roughly where she lived, but Lexie had never invited her over to her place — which now seemed strange. When she arrived, she cautiously approached the little house and knocked on the door. Lexie answered, clearly surprised to see Mina.

"What are you doing here?" she grunted.

"I brought you some soup." Mina held up the container of soup.

"What for?"

"Because you're sick . . . aren't you?" Mina asked. Aside from looking exhausted, Mina could tell that Lexie wasn't sick — at least not with a cold or flu.

"Right," Lexie replied, stepping out of the house and onto the front porch. She closed the door behind her as if she didn't want Mina to see inside or get any ideas about being invited in. "You should have called first."

"Would you have answered?" Mina clapped back.

"Of course, if I wasn't . . ." Lexie trailed off.

"Wasn't what? What's going on?" Mina demanded.

Lexie pinched the bridge of her nose and sighed.

"Look, if you want to break up with me, then just do it. Don't ghost me and leave me wondering what went wrong!" Mina shouted, unable to stop herself from spiralling.

Lexie reached out and grabbed Mina's hands, her eyes wide with worry.

"That's not what I'm doing."

Mina was still angry. She would settle for nothing but the truth.

"Then tell me what's going on," she demanded.

Lexie sighed. Relenting, she opened the door to her house, inviting Mina inside.

14 Secrets

MINA STEPPED INSIDE, unsure of what she would find beyond the front door. A mafia boss holding Lexie and her family hostage, a portal to an alternate universe where the real Lexie was stuck after swapping places with the Lexie in front of her now, or maybe a film crew ready to leap out and tell her that her first relationship was just an elaborate prank. But what she found was a very normal home. Lexie led her into the kitchen where a young boy was sitting at the table building a LEGO tower.

"Who are you?" he asked suspiciously as Mina entered. Mina looked to Lexie, unsure if she was allowed to answer him.

"I'm Mina," she replied.

"Mina?" the boy screeched and jumped up. "*You're* Mina! Lexie talks about you all the time! I'm Zac, her brother. She's probably told you all about me."

"She sure has," Mina lied, not wanting to squash his excitement.

"Zac, lower your voice. Grams is asleep," Lexie scolded.

"Oh, I'm up now," a trembling voice came from behind them. Mina turned to see Lexie's grandmother, a white-haired woman in pyjamas, pulling an oxygen tank behind her. Lexie rushed to her side, and Grams waved her off gently. "Oh, I'm all right." She slowly made her way to the kitchen table and sat down. "Mina, is it? It's so nice to finally meet you."

Mina shook her hand and smiled. "You too."

"Lexie dear, why don't you fix us some tea. Mina, you come sit."

They did as they were told. Grams and Zac were very excited to get to know Mina. They asked her all about her life. How did she like working at the mall? Where did she grow up? How long had she known Lexie? How did they meet?

Mina answered all their questions, but she could see that Lexie didn't have the same level of excitement as they did. They sat for about an hour, sipping their tea and chatting, until Grams felt like she needed to lie down. Lexie helped her to her room, and Zac took Mina to the living room to show her his LEGO collection. She looked at the wall full of family photos: Lexie starting elementary school, Zac in a basketball uniform, a nice photo of the three of them in a garden — but not a single photo of their mother or father.

Lexie came into the living room and told Zac that he'd better finish up his tower. He whined a little but went back to the kitchen table and continued his work. Mina let Lexie lead her back out to the front porch, where they stood in silence, neither knowing where to begin.

"Why didn't you tell me that your grandmother was sick?" Mina finally asked.

"It's not that I didn't want you to know about her. I just . . ." Lexie paused and Mina waited, letting her gather her thoughts. "My life is very different than yours, and my future is uncertain at best."

"What do you mean?"

"You're going off to college in a few weeks. Your life is moving forward, and I'll still be here, working full-time at the mall and looking after my grandmother and my brother."

"Why do you have to look after your grandmother and little brother? Where are your parents? I mean, you talk about your mom. I just assumed they were around . . ."

"I talk about memories I have of her. There was a time when my mom was around, but she moved to BC with her new boyfriend a few years ago, and we don't hear from her much. Dad was never really in the picture." Lexie spoke in a matter-of-fact tone, but Mina could tell there was a deep well of pain just beneath the surface. She took a deep breath and took Lexie's hand, but Lexie pulled away from her. "I don't want your pity."

"I don't pity you," Mina muttered, shocked by Lexie's tone. "I can see you're struggling, and I care about you. I want to help. That's what partners do."

"Look, I don't know if I can be your partner anymore. After dinner with your folks, I realized that I might not be what's best for you."

"How could you say that? You make me so happy," Mina challenged her.

"For now maybe, but what are things going to be like when you're at school? How will I fit into your life then when we aren't working together all the time?"

"We'll figure it out. It's not like I'm moving away. We'll still see each other all the time."

"No, you don't get it. Our lives are on two different paths, and mine is going nowhere fast. I don't think I can give you the kind of future you want." Lexie shook her head.

"I want a future with you," Mina said with all the conviction she could muster, but Lexie was lost.

"Eventually you're going to realize that I'm not enough, and you'll leave. I'm just saving us from an even deeper heartache down the road," Lexie murmured.

Mina could tell that a rift had come between them, and no matter what she said, she wouldn't be able to reach Lexie. Mina held back her tears, but nodded.

"Okay," she muttered. She pressed her forehead against Lexie's shoulder and squeezed her arm. Neither said goodbye as Mina stood up and returned to her car. She couldn't help but look back over her shoulder. She caught sight of Lexie wiping her face with her sleeve and going back inside the house. Her father's words rang in her ears: *The occasional argument just means that you're invested in the relationship. It means you care about someone enough to try to get through hard times or uncomfortable situations.* The fact that Lexie didn't fight for their relationship at all meant she didn't care about Mina anymore.

Mina sat in the car for what felt like an eternity, letting herself cry. She finally put it into drive and went home. She went straight to her room and curled up in her bed. When her father called her down for dinner, she told him she wasn't feeling well and wanted to stay in bed. Later, he brought up a plate of food and took her temperature. He must have known that she wasn't sick, but he didn't pry. He simply kissed her forehead and reminded her that he was there for her if she needed him.

That night, Mina tossed and turned. She couldn't sleep. Her mind was a rollercoaster ranging from sad, to angry, to numb. She didn't know how to feel. When she realized that sleep wasn't going to happen, she decided to do what she always did when she was upset. She grabbed her phone, opened her Pinterest app, and created a new board called "Reminders." Then she proceeded to search and pin pictures and videos that made her feel better: travel photos, inspirational quotes, funny dog memes, and recipes. Anything and everything that would either distract her or bring a smile to her face when she looked at it.

She continued to scroll through her phone. She visited Instagram against her better judgement and came across Luscious Lingerie's post about their employee photo contest.

Maybe I should do it, she thought, considering whether or not it would actually make her feel better. *Going with the flow is easier than going against it.* She wished she could rewind her summer and go back to when everything seemed glittery and hopeful. When she and Lexie were just starting to flirt, and shopping was a fun activity and not a guilt-ridden, aimless pastime that contributed to fast-fashion, and working at Luscious Lingerie felt like a status symbol and not a grind. But she couldn't. Her blinders had been torn off, and now she saw things how they really were. What was the solution? Mina didn't know.

15 Broken Hearts

WHEN HER ALARM WENT OFF at 5:15 a.m., Mina was already awake. She rolled out of bed and thought about calling in sick. Heartache was as good a reason as any, she supposed. But she knew she'd just spend the whole day in bed and wind up feeling worse than she did already. Plus, Monica would no doubt call her in the afternoon and try to get her to come in anyway; "Just bring some tissues," she would say. So Mina forced herself to brush her teeth, tied her curly black hair up in a messy bun, and threw on the first black outfit she could find. Her dad was downstairs and ready to go. He offered her a muffin, which she ate despite feeling sick to her stomach. The drive to work was silent. Aaron, the security guard, let her into the mall and her dad waved goodbye, watching to make sure she got inside safely.

"Hey, Mina," Aaron said hopefully. Mina didn't reply. She just gave him a nod, then walked through the mall towards Luscious Lingerie.

Much to Mina's dismay, Lexie was at work and was waiting outside the store with everyone else. Em unlocked the doors, and they went inside to start their day. Mina held back tears the entire shift, trying not to make eye contact or stand too close to Lexie. Chase, Madison, and Yui knew something was up but didn't want to cause any drama, so they kept to themselves until it came time to run product to the floor. Chase followed Mina with a handful of bras and stopped her near the front of the store, away from everyone else.

"Hey, are you okay?" they asked.

"If I talk about it, I'll cry, so . . ." Mina whispered, shaking her head and holding back the tears.

"Okay . . ." Chase said, panicking. "I bought the underwear with the non-binary flag on them."

"You did?" Mina asked, surprised.

"Yup. I feel ashamed and excited. Stupid capitalist society making me pay for my own label," they joked. Their attempt to distract Mina worked. She smiled and couldn't help but chuckle. "I'll take the small joys where I can get them and remind myself that it won't always be like this. Things will get better." Chase gave her arm a squeeze. "Besides, when the revolution comes, this place will be the first to go." Chase laughed with Mina then walked off into a different section of the store.

Mina finished running her handful of product and caught Lexie watching her from across the store. She kept her head down until the sales staff started to arrive. Then she found Monica and asked about being transferred to the sales team.

"Are you kidding me? We would love to have you!" Monica beamed. "I'll talk to Em and get things sorted out."

Em was reluctant to let Mina go but agreed. Monica moved Mina to the sales floor for the rest of her shift. It was hard to be away from Lexie, but it was even harder to be working next to her. *This is for the best*, Mina thought. Ultimately, she didn't want to be in a relationship with someone who didn't want to be with her. Mina spent the rest of her day cleaning the panty table and helping customers. She even agreed to stay late so she wouldn't have to check out at the same time as Lexie. After the merchandising team left for the day, Mina felt like she could finally relax.

"I heard about you and Lexie." Tia, another sales associate, came to help her clean up the panty table. "I'm really sorry, that sucks."

"Oh. Yeah, thanks," Mina replied. She didn't expect anyone to know so fast.

"It's too bad. I thought you two were really good for each other. Or at least you were good for Lexie."

"Were you two friends?" Mina asked. She and Tia had never really talked outside of work.

"No, but we started together and used to grab

lunch from time to time. We're work acquaintances, I guess."

"Oh."

"She's a tough cookie, that Lexie. I hope her grandmother is feeling better."

"You know about her grandmother?"

"Yeah, she was just telling me about her." Tia shrugged, folding another pair of panties.

"Huh," Mina scoffed, annoyed.

"What?" Tia asked.

"Nothing. It's just . . . I can't believe she told you about her grandmother and not me. I didn't even know she existed until yesterday, when Lexie broke up with me. No offence, but you said it yourself, you're not even friends," Mina exclaimed, exasperated. Everything she'd been keeping inside started to spill out of her.

"Yeah, but sometimes it's harder to be honest and vulnerable with the people you care about. There's no fear of judgement confiding in a stranger — or a work acquaintance." Tia chuckled. "I mean, what am I going to say aside from 'Aw that sucks, I hope things get better soon.' I don't have any obligation to help out or get involved or ask about what she's doing."

"So, what, you think she's upset because I found out and offered to help?" Mina replied, confused and frustrated.

"I don't know, but Lexie strikes me as someone who doesn't think past tomorrow. She's always scrambling to take care of things, or other people. I don't think she really knows how to let anyone look after her. You know?"

Mina watched Tia tuck a perfectly folded pair of panties into a drawer and thought about what she'd said. Monica called Tia to the cash, and she left Mina alone at the panty table once again. *This is so confusing*, Mina thought. *I don't know if I should reach out or back off.*

She found herself thinking about the very fibre of her character and reflected on her actions from the day before. *Who am I?* She stopped folding when she noticed two young girls looking around the store. She was about to ask them if they needed any help when she caught them admiring the huge poster in the front section of the store. It featured a thin, chiseled model with photoshopped smoothed skin, perfectly curled hair, large breasts, and no stomach whatsoever. Mina watched, horrified, as the girls looked at their stomachs, sucked in, and tried to pose like the model.

She looked around the room at all the posters, each one showing a woman that looked like a cookie-cutter version of the last. Maybe it was the breakup, maybe it was the lack of sleep, but Mina was questioning everything. *Is this who I am? Am I okay with this? How am I actually helping other women feel good about themselves? Can I do that even when I don't feel good about myself? Why does it feel like everything's falling apart?*

Her mind was swarmed with questions she didn't have any answers to, and of course the one person she wanted to talk to was Lexie.

Monica approached and noticed her eyeing the two young girls.

"So cute," she murmured. "It's good to get them while they're young, then they're Luscious customers for life!" Monica beamed. Mina was mortified.

Suddenly, her out-of-control world that felt like it had been spinning non-stop for weeks stood absolutely still.

"I quit," Mina said calmly.

"What?" Monica looked at her, confused.

"I quit!" Mina yelled, drawing some attention from customers and employees alike.

"Excuse me?" Monica clutched her chest in embarrassment and frustration. "But this is not how you resign. We require two weeks' notice —"

"No you don't. Two weeks' notice is a courtesy that *I* can provide for *you*, but I don't feel like being very courteous. Especially since I've worked more double shifts than I can count for crap wages at the biggest insecurity factory in the world!"

Mina looked around the room. "This shit isn't even nice!" She picked up a pair of panties off the table and threw them over her shoulder. She picked up another and tossed it, then another, and another. "Everything pills in the wash, or it shrinks, and it's made of cheap, non-sustainable materials that either need to be replaced every few months or break apart on their own! And why? Because you're trying to convince us that owning the newest bra and panty set will make us feel good about ourselves. But you're not helping women. You're hurting them. And I'm not going to be a part of that anymore."

Monica's jaw dropped. The floor surrounding Mina was covered in panties and everyone in the store was staring at her. In her final moment of triumph, Mina marched over to the two young girls who, like everyone else, were watching the scene unfold in front of them. "Get out while you can," she warned them. "I'm not saying that it's wrong to look this way, or even that it's wrong to care about how you look. But this . . . this is not the be-all and end-all of beauty. Despite what they're telling you — what it feels like everyone is telling you — you don't need to look like this. Or to spend money on this cheap fast-fashion crap. You are so much more than how you look." The two girls stared at Mina in surprise, unsure how to respond.

"Now wait one minute," Monica shrieked, finally regaining her ability to speak. She followed Mina, stammering and scolding, all the way to the break room, where Mina calmly gathered her things.

Monica proceeded to throw a tantrum and refused to check Mina out. Em had to step in and do it.

"You sure about this?" Em asked. "We'd love to have you back on the merch team."

"Yeah, I'm sure." Mina nodded. She flung her purse over her shoulder and headed out of the store.

"Hey!" Lexie called, chasing after her. "Wait!" Mina stopped outside the store, and the two stood face to face in the bustling mall.

"I . . . I thought you'd left already," Mina stammered, embarrassed.

"I agreed to stay late and help Em in the back," Lexie explained.

"Oh," Mina replied. She hadn't known Lexie was around to see her outburst. They stood in painful silence as the mall bustled around them.

"You're not quitting because of me, are you?" Lexie blurted out.

"No." Mina sighed. She couldn't look Lexie in the eye.

"I don't want to be the reason you're leaving," Lexie said.

"You're not. Believe me, that had nothing to do with you." Adrenaline was coursing through her. "I just — Everyone is trying to tell me who I should be, and I can't take it anymore. I'm done with anything and anyone who *tells* me who I am instead of just *asking* me. I might still be figuring some things out, but I know that this . . ." She gestured to the huge ad in the store window. "This isn't me. I thought I could ignore it and be a part of something that would make me feel better about myself, but it's mostly had the opposite effect, and I can't look the other way anymore."

"Wow. Yeah, I get it," Lexie replied.

"I wish you could quit too, but . . ." Mina sighed.

"I don't want to quit," Lexie snapped.

"You've been telling me since I started that you hate so much about what this brand represents —"

"Okay, yes, but I also like the work I do, and the people I work with. Don't forget about them. Not to mention the fact that I couldn't quit even if I wanted to. I can't afford it."

"Right," Mina said. They stood in silence for a moment.

"I guess . . ." Lexie cut herself off. "Never mind."

"I'll see you around?" Mina replied. Lexie just nodded.

Mina walked away from Luscious Lingerie. What had started out feeling like a triumphant moment was beginning to contain the sinking feeling of regret.

Mina took the bus home and thought about Lexie the entire ride. *I guess in a way I do pity her*, she silently confessed. *Why else would I have said that I wish she could quit if I didn't think she was somehow stuck there?* She thought about how she could have handled that differently, but the pain of their breakup was still fresh, and thinking about her too much only made her sad.

Mina got off the bus and shuffled home, dragging her feet as she approached the house. She came to the realization that she would have to tell her parents she quit her job.

16 Family Values

MINA SAT HER PARENTS DOWN in the living room and told them that she'd quit her job.

"What?" her mother exclaimed. "I did not raise a quitter! What did they do to you that was so bad, huh?"

"Nothing, I just . . . I decided that it wasn't a good fit for me."

"Some jobs are hard, but you can't quit just because things get tough," her father added calmly.

"Things didn't get 'tough.' I just realized that my values didn't align with theirs."

"We do not quit. We work hard and we persevere. How do you expect to get anywhere in life if you quit when things get tough? What about your tuition?" her mother continued.

"I've saved enough for my first semester. I'll find another part-time job for fall and —"

"This isn't like you, Mina." Voula shook her head and paced on the carpet.

"Ma, can't you just trust that I know what's best for me?" Mina exclaimed.

"You are too young to know what's best for you. You should have talked to me first," her mother lamented.

"What's going on?" Alexandra asked cautiously as she and Dimitri poked their heads into the living room.

"Nothing!" Mina yelled. "God! Not everything I do needs to become a family ordeal! Just back off and let me figure things out!"

She'd had it. She stormed up to her room and slammed the door, which she instantly regretted. She heard her mother stomping around in the living room and yelling up to her. She felt tears welling in her eyes. She felt bad fighting with her parents, but she didn't know how else to deal with them in this moment. She slumped down onto the bed and covered her face with her hands. There was a knock at the door.

"Go away!" Mina yelled.

"Can we come in?" Alexandra called through the door. Mina sat up. *Alexandra?* Mina opened her door a crack and saw Alexandra and Dimitri waiting outside. She opened the door all the way, letting them in, and sat back down on the bed. Dimitri closed the door behind them and sat down next to her.

"You okay?" Alexandra asked.

"Obviously not," Dimitri replied for her. Alexandra smacked his shoulder and sat on Mina's other side.

"What's going on?" Alexandra asked. Mina sighed and told them everything. How devastating her breakup with Lexie had been. How she started to feel bad about herself being inundated with the environment at work. How her boss was pushing her to apply to this contest. And just how frustrated she was not meeting everyone's expectations.

"Wow. Heavy," Dimitri muttered.

"I get it," Alexandra said after a moment of silence.

"Do you?" Mina raised an eyebrow at her perfect older sister.

"Yes!" Alexandra exclaimed. "There's just so much pressure to be . . . perfect. Or do something great —"

"To make Mom and Dad proud," Dimitri interrupted.

Alexandra continued. "And it comes from everywhere, not just parents . . . from teachers, friends, the Internet. Don't get me wrong, sometimes I need someone to push me, but most of the time, I just want someone to tell me that what I'm doing is okay. "

"Even if all you're doing today is just existing," Dimitri added.

"Yeah," Alexandra agreed. "Not everything has to be about racing forward. Sometimes it's nice just to be in the present and be okay with where you are in that moment."

"I didn't know you two felt that way," Mina said.

"Of course we do," Dimitri exclaimed. "What, you thought we were robots?"

This made Mina laugh. She did kind of think of her siblings as otherworldly. "Yeah, something like that," she joked. "Thank you."

"No problem, sis." Alexandra put her arm around her and pulled her into a hug, which Dimitri reluctantly joined. "Give Mom some time. She'll be over it by tomorrow. Just like when I quit my trumpet lessons."

"You played the trumpet?" Mina cocked her head to the side, trying to remember a time when there was trumpet music in the house. Alexandra held up her hand in a halting motion.

"We don't speak of it," she replied. They laughed, and Dimitri told the story of how Alexandra was forced to practice in the basement because she was so bad, but Mom wouldn't let her quit, until one day she threw the trumpet and broke it. Mina laughed, finally remembering the tragic scene of the broken trumpet. Dimitri ruffled her hair, and they left her alone in her room once again. But now she felt much better about everything. More than that — they made her feel normal, like everything she was feeling was just part of growing up. *I guess it is*, she thought.

***

Alexandra was right: the next day, their mother had gotten over the shock of Mina quitting her job and apologized for her reaction. Mina forgave her and told her about the breakup and how she'd been feeling at work lately. Her mother jumped into fix-it mode and encouraged her to start dating again, then promptly asked to take her shopping for *better* clothes. Mina calmly and courageously said no.

"I'm okay, Ma. You don't have to worry about my love life, my future, or my clothes. Yeah, I'm feeling sad about the breakup, but it's okay for me to be sad about it for a while. At the end of the day, I like the way I look, and I like Lexie. I'm not ready to move on yet," Mina explained.

"I just want you to be happy," Voula pressed.

"Then you need to accept that I can be happy on my own. All this talk about having a partner makes me feel like I can only be happy in a relationship — which just isn't true. I like spending time alone, and I have lots of great relationships in my life that aren't romantic."

Her mother considered this and embraced her. "Oh, my love, I'm sorry," she said. "What can I do to make it up to you?"

"You know, sometimes I just need you to listen to me. I don't always need you to tell me what to do next or come up with a solution."

"I'll try my best." Her mother nodded. "Except when I know one hundred percent that you are wrong and I am right, okay?"

"Okay." Mina laughed. "And another thing . . . I need you to stop commenting on my body and my weight. Good or bad. I know that you mean well, but you have to understand that it hurts me. Deeply."

Voula kissed Mina's cheeks. "Okay, I will try. I know sometimes I push too much. I used to hate it when my mother did the same thing." She laughed in spite of herself. "I love you."

"I love you too, Mom."

It felt good to talk to her mother, and while she suspected that any change to come would be slow, she appreciated that she'd been heard. Mina decided to change the subject and asked for her mother's help picking out her fall semester courses, which Voula was only too happy to help with. With only two weeks left until the beginning of the school year, Mina was starting to feel excited about this next chapter.

17 Closure

EVERY NOW AND AGAIN, the anxiety snake would coil in Mina's chest or hiss in her ear and make her think about Lexie and the way things had ended. But she would unravel its knots and refocus on what she could control. She thought about reaching out to Lexie, telling her that she missed her and that she was thinking about her. But she didn't want to seem desperate or pushy, since Lexie was the one who ended things. One night, after Mina posted a picture on Instagram of her and Chase hanging out at a coffee shop, Lexie texted her.

Lexie: Hey. How are you?

Mina: Hi! I'm okay, how are you?

Lexie: I'm good. Grams is doing a lot better.

Mina: That's great! I'm so glad.

Lexie: Yeah me too.

Mina: I miss you.

Lexie: I miss you too.

Lexie: I still think this is for the best tho. You're going to start school soon and you'll probably meet someone better than me. Someone who won't hold you back.

Mina: You never held me back.

Lexie didn't reply after that, and Mina decided not to push it. The more she thought about Lexie, the more she realized that the breakup wasn't about her. Lexie was grappling with her own expectations and pressures. It made Mina feel both relieved and sad that Lexie was struggling with the same thing she was.

The next day, Mina reached out again. She'd thought about it all night long, and she needed to tell Lexie how she felt and get some closure. Mina realized that expecting Lexie to fight for their relationship might have been what she wanted, but not something that Lexie could do — especially if she didn't see a future together. Lexie agreed to meet for coffee at a place near Mina's house. Mina tried not to put too much effort into her hair and makeup, but she was secretly thrilled to be seeing Lexie again.

Before she walked into the coffee shop, Mina reminded herself, *You're not here to get back together. You're just here to apologize and get some closure.* Lexie walked in, and they ordered coffees together, each paying for their own, then found a cozy place to sit and chat. After some obligatory small talk, they sat in silence, staring at one another.

"You look good," Lexie said suddenly.

"You too," Mina replied.

"Been getting ready for school?" Lexie asked.

"Yeah, I picked out my courses and registered online."

"That's great."

"I'm really happy to see you," Mina blurted out.

Lexie blushed and tucked her hair behind her ears. "I'm happy to see you too," she replied.

"I'm sorry about the comment I made the day I left work. About how I wished you could quit too. I was just thinking about myself."

"It's okay. I'm sorry I didn't tell you about my family. I should have just told you, but after dinner with your folks things just felt really serious between us and . . . I already felt like I wasn't good enough for you," Lexie confessed.

Mina reached across the small coffee table between them and took Lexie's hand. This time she didn't pull away. They sat for a moment in silence, the clatter and bustle of the cafe swirling around them as they looked at each other longingly.

"I'm sorry I didn't tell you when we were together, but you are amazing," Mina said. "You're brave, generous, and kind. You have always been more than good enough."

Lexie squeezed her hand, and tears welled in her eyes. "I really messed this up, didn't I?" she mumbled.

Mina chuckled and shook her head. "No. You don't want to be with me, and yes, that hurts, but it's all right that we want different things. I just wanted to tell you that there's no hard feelings on my end. I'm really glad I got to know you. I still care about you a lot."

"Mina —"

"Seriously! God, if you could peek inside my stomach and see the butterflies that you give me . . ." They laughed. "But that's not why we're here —"

"Would you take me back?" Lexie asked.

"In a heartbeat." Mina nodded. She tried to keep the excitement in her voice to a minimum.

Lexie wiped away a tear. "Even though I shut down when I get upset?"

"Communication will just be something we have to work on," Mina countered.

"And I have a shitty job at an underwear store that barely pays minimum wage?"

"You're one of the smartest and most hardworking people I know. You'll succeed there or anywhere else you want," Mina said.

"What about the fact that I think golden doodles are overrated?"

"That I didn't know about. And yes, it is a deal breaker." Mina held a serious look as long as she could before they both burst into laughter. The butterflies in Mina's stomach multiplied, and each flutter made her happier and happier. "You wanna get out of here? I know a place that makes the *best* chocolate ice cream in the city."

Lexie smiled and nodded. "Oh! I have to be home by six to make sure Grams takes her medication." She sighed.

"Why don't we pick up ice cream for Zac and Grams too? We can sit on the porch together," Mina suggested.

"Are you sure? Mina, I don't want you to feel like you have to share in my responsibilities —"

"It's no trouble, seriously. Besides, your family loves me!" Mina chimed.

Lexie laughed. "That's true."

"Great. Let's take things slow, we don't have to —"
But before Mina could finish her thought, Lexie pulled
her in for a kiss. It was electric. Mina felt like she might
explode, she was so happy. She held Lexie's face close
to hers. She couldn't stop kissing her. Finally, Lexie
pulled away, still holding Mina's hand and smiling so
wide Mina worried that her face might crack. They left
the cafe together, hand in hand, as the late afternoon
sun just started to dip below the horizon.

18 Sunshine Ahead

TWO WEEKS LATER, as the last weekend of summer break snuck up on them, Lexie and Mina made plans to go to the beach. The last two weeks had been incredible. Their families had a wonderful dinner together, Lexie started to open up about her past, and they'd even had a couple of arguments which they managed to resolve without incident. Mina knew they were riding the high of getting back together, but something felt different. Mina was more confident, more in tune with herself, more secure. She shared the Pinterest board she'd made during their breakup, and together they filled it with reminders of self-love, travel destinations, and dreams for the future. Both felt hopeful and emboldened by their growing love for one another.

Lexie picked Mina up after she'd finished work, and Mina could tell that she was about to burst with news. Lexie kissed Mina softly on the lips and waited patiently for her to put on her seat belt.

"Okay, what's going on? You're practically vibrating." Mina laughed.

"I got an interview!" Lexie exclaimed

"Yeah, you do!" Mina cheered, hugging Lexie across the centre console of the car. "I'm so proud of you!"

"Thanks! I'm so excited! It's such a cool little start-up. I mean, the job is pretty straight forward — SEOs, web design, some other back-end maintenance, but your dad said they've got big plans. I have to get your dad a thank-you gift," Lexie rambled.

"You don't have to do that," Mina replied.

"Yes, I do!"

"No, you don't!" Mina laughed at her excitement. "He just sent you the job posting."

"He checked out some of my work and he's going to help me prep for the interview. I'll make him a card. Oh! And I'll get him some *dee-las* — is that it?"

"Diples," Mina corrected, referring to the crisp, honey-soaked Greek dessert.

"His favourite," Lexie confirmed.

"He'd love that," Mina relented. They drove through the subdivision, out onto the highway, and eventually down the winding coastal road to the beach. Lexie continued to beam and excitedly talked about the job. It seemed that Mina's dad had come around to the idea that experience and hard work might be the same path to success for others as well. He and Lexie could talk endlessly about technology at their family dinners. Lexie admitted that she would be sad to leave the merch team, but Mina reminded her that they would all still hang out with Chase, Madison, and Yui. After all, good work friends are what make a retail job bearable.

When they arrived at the beach, they unpacked the car and picked out the perfect spot to set up their towels and umbrella. The warm sun beamed down on the beachgoers, and a cool ocean breeze whipped around them. It was the perfect day to be by the sea. Lexie immediately started to take off her coverup, the dark blue lapping water calling to her. Mina joined her. She took off her shorts and t-shirt, stripping down to her bikini. Lexie was about to run to the water when Mina pulled out her phone.

"Wait! I want a picture first." Mina held her phone out and snapped a selfie of the two of them together.

"All right, I'm going!" And with that Lexie took off toward the water. Mina looked at the photo; she noticed the rolls in her stomach, the stretch marks, the cellulite, and the huge smile plastered across her face. Without a second thought she posted the picture to her Instagram, captioning it with a couple of beach emojis, and tucked her phone into her bag. Then she ran into the water, where Lexie was waiting for her with open arms and a mischievous grin.

ACKNOWLEDGEMENTS

First and foremost, I want to thank my loving and supportive parents, Melody and John Bakolias — everything I am I owe to you and your endless care and attention. Thank you for being so supportive when I came out as queer, and for always encouraging my artistic pursuits.

Thank you to my partner Benjamin Hayes for supporting my work and loving me as I am.

Thank you to Allister Thompson, Heather Epp, Morgan Wright, James Lorimer, and the entire Lorimer team for your support, feedback and for the opportunity to write.

Lastly, thank you to Shannon, Maggie, Joanna, Megan, Jenna, Naz, Brittney, Linden, Hannah, Caitlin, Stacey, Katie, Jailee, Alex, Nina, Emily, Deb, Amy, Subrina, Janika, Jasmine, Kandice, Shekara, Lauren, Meaghan, Homa, Elsie, Dot, Dina, Jocelyn, Allison, and Emma. It was the best of times, it was the worst of times, but getting to know you made it worth it.